DARKENED
WATERS

Also by Gary Lee Vincent

Novels
PASSAGEWAY

Darkened – The West Virginia Vampire Series
DARKENED HILLS
DARKENED HOLLOWS
DARKENED WATERS
DARKENED SOULS

Nonfiction
THE WINNER, THE LOSER
AGELATIONS
CONFIGURATION MANAGEMENT

Musical Releases
100 PERCENT
PASSION, PLEASURE, & PAIN
SOMEWHERE DOWN THE ROAD

DARKENED WATERS

GARY LEE VINCENT

Burning Bulb
PUBLISHING

Darkened Waters
By **Gary Lee Vincent**

Burning Bulb Publishing
P.O. Box 4721
Bridgeport, WV 26330-4721
www.BurningBulbPublishing.com

PUBLISHER'S NOTE: This book is a work of fiction. Names, characters, places, and incidents are either the product of the author's imagination or are used fictitiously, and any resemblance to actual persons, living or dead, events, or locales is purely coincidental.

Edition ISBN

Paperback 978-0-61562-351-1

First edition.
Printed in the United States of America.

Library of Congress Control Number: 2012936563

Dedicated to:

YOU

INTRODUCTION

When *Darkened Hills* first came along, I knew it was something special. People seem to like vampire stories and the first book had just the right mix of familiarity and local craziness to deliver a pretty good entertainment "punch." Author Joey Madia called it a "Vampire Pastiche" and its subsequent success after its release as *ForeWord Review Magazine's* 2010 Book of the Year for top horror novel by an Independent Press really helped to set the stage for the *DARKENED* series, the third installment of which you now hold.

And just as *Darkened Hills* was my pastiche tribute to the great vampire works of *Dracula, 'salem's Lot,* and the like, *Darkened Hollows* intentionally set out to introduce the spiritual realm of dark forces that plague the vampire mystique and in doing so, took the story from a core event centered around a small town, to a far greater age-old battle that our small group of heroes are now caught up in.

I personally have always thought of Bram Stoker's *Dracula* as one of the first Western novels – a group of unlikely heroes heading out into the wild frontier to dispense justice. Thus, I suppose that this was in the back of my conscience as this "Western" feel casts its shadow against the overarching storyline in the *DARKENED* novels – the exception being that our heroes are not in the Wild West, per say, but Wild West Virginia.

So, as all hell breaks loose in *Darkened Hollows* we are now faced with an inevitable climax that must now play out in Book III – *Darkened Waters.*

In the time of the Great Flood, the Bible recounts that the world would not be destroyed again by water as it was in the days of Noah. But as our heroes (and you, Dear Reader) are about to discover, millions of gallons of water can still set the stage for the evil that is about to come forth.

Get ready, Dear Reader, and head for higher ground as we begin *Darkened Waters...*

ACKNOWLEDGEMENTS

A sincere appreciation goes out to the following people, whom without there tireless efforts to keep up with my demented mind, this book (and series) could not have been as polished as it ended up.

I would like to first thank my content editors Linda Innes – for providing technical expertise, research, and character psychological insight; Madeleine Swann – for her input on an erotica throwback for the setting of the events surrounding the Salem Witch Trials of the late 1600s; and to George Cunningham, whose input on narrative strategy and overarching plots really added to the suspense of what makes a *DARKENED* book great.

Next, I would like to thank my copy editors Joey Madia and Rich Bottles, Jr. for their keen eye in helping me correct my sloppiness. They found quite a few things early on so you could appreciate the read now. Any errors that you find in this final run are solely my fault as they did a tremendous job proofing the manuscript.

Finally, thank you, Dear Reader, for sticking with me and supporting freedom of speech and the small press. You are the reason I do what I do.

PROLOGUE

Isabella drifted carefully into the shadows of the trees when she heard a branch crack in the bushes. She gripped the bowl of dried plants tightly, ready to throw them if caught. The footfalls headed in her direction over the fallen leaves, once a myriad of color but now a dejected brown. She heard her name called softly and released her breath when she recognized Mary's voice. "I saw you hide in the trees," laughed the girl quietly; gripping her basket of pinecones, acorns, and fragrant herbs.

They picked their way carefully through the mud, the sweet smelling blackberries, and heavy musk of the undergrowth clinging to their shawls. Isabella felt stirrings of panic, certain they had arrived on the wrong day as the sun was slowly hidden by the canopy. When voices and the crackle of campfire drifted towards them she felt her body relax, and the two girls exchanged excited glances. They picked up the pace and soon stood in a clearing where several women giggled and chattered. A great fire leapt into the air and baskets and clay bowls containing various offerings of dried seeds and nuts, leaves and bread were stashed in the middle. The fluttering in Isabella's stomach was familiar but just as strong as the first time, and she surreptitiously wiped her sweating hands on her dress.

"We have brought gifts for the Mabon Equinox, to give thanks and to release our old cares and grievances," announced Anne, standing apart from the others. Her blue eyes surveyed the watching women and her quiet confidence immediately drew all attention to her. Her poise had always made Isabella nervous, and she had often found herself becoming flustered and speaking too fast in her presence. Now, though, she was content to watch her urging the women to pick up a basket and scatter the contents amongst the trees. Isabella dutifully did so, weaving through the figures as they flung offerings with an abandon never exhibited around the reserved townsfolk.

Isabella caught up with Mary and the two fell in theatrical exhaustion next to the fire. Others followed in the familiar ritual, flopping onto the springy earth in a play of innocence while lying as closely to the others as possible. Isabella was always too afraid to advance first but she soon felt fingertips stroking her ankle. In response she felt the warmth and wetness between her legs and reached out to caress Mary's stomach. She had always loved the feel of it; it wasn't the smoothest or the softest skin, but it felt the most comfortable. The fingertips below tickled their way from her ankle to her thigh and she parted her legs to ease their path. Her eyes snuck over the others and noticed Alyssia's breasts already bare, wood-smoke caressing her hair and May Jones sucking at her nipple.

Soft sighs surrounded her, including Mary's as she reached down her smock and felt for her heavy breasts. The fingertips on Isabella's thigh crept upwards to nestle in her undergarments, rifling through the material to find their destination. They ran gently over her wet lips as Isabella placed her own mouth over Mary's freed breast. She rolled her tongue over the pointed nipple, earning a satisfied groan from the other girl. Isabella moaned herself when the fingers at her private lips found their mark, gently circling the spot that made her body as hot as fire.

She watched as one of the writhing bodies lowered her head between Mary's legs, and she turned to face Isabella. The two girls smiled self-consciously before Mary moaned, almost surprised afterwards at her own reaction.

Isabella felt herself growing hotter at the sight of Mary rocking her hips to the other girl's tongue, a small wave rolling over her body as a sigh came from her mouth. Mary reached for Isabella and pulled down the front of her dress, tugging and teasing at her erect nipples.

"Tug harder," urged Isabella and Mary obliged. Their eyes met again and this time they didn't look away, watching intently while the sensation built up further and higher and they both called "Oh," and Isabella watched Mary's pupils dilate.

She lay still a moment, the bodies around her swapping and stroking and rolling, until something made her glance upwards; a twig snapped. She instinctively covered her breasts when she noticed a figure standing apart from the women, a male figure wearing a crown. She squinted; there was a peculiarity to him but she was unsure why. She rose slowly, stepping over the mass of pleasure, and walked towards him. She realized his skin was strange, that it seemed to glow in the shifting firelight.

He waited patiently for her to reach him, smiling calmly. Isabella put her hand out to touch his face, running her fingers over his cheeks. He seemed so familiar; she felt a years-old ache for a boy in the village who hadn't returned her love. Here he was, strange and beautiful, but – she narrowed her eyes and saw he was not whom she had thought. Something though – something in his features had ignited the same need and frustration. She kissed him, biting his lip gently. "Have you waited for me long?" he whispered. Isabella nodded, feeling the hairs rise over her body.

He led her to a tree nearby and leaned her against it. "Let me see you," he said, the urgency in his voice bringing fresh excitement. Improvising, she lifted her dress up to her waist and exposed her private area. It felt like the most daring thing she had ever done and she couldn't help glancing sideways to ensure nobody else could see. He stepped nearer and extended his hand towards her thighs, running his fingertips upwards. She parted her legs without question, her mouth slightly open and her private place waiting impatiently. Gently his digit caressed the outer lips; she knew she should refuse him, be outraged, but instead she let him slide his finger inside her. He reached as far as he could go before crooking it slowly forwards, tickling her furthermost point and drawing a long moan. He repeated the action as he unbuckled himself, releasing his erection. In curiosity Isabella leaned down, wrapping her fingers around the shaft and wondering at its subsequent pulsing. He appeared to take pleasure from it, so, without forethought, she knelt down to enact a deed the townsfolk would have branded her for.

Leaning on her knees with her hands still gripping his shaft, she faltered nervously. Her eyes flicked upwards to his and he nodded his encouragement. Her husband would never have allowed her to do this despite the idea sneaking into her mind on more than one night. She stuck her tongue out and experimentally licked the tip, growing in confidence when he moaned appreciatively and placed a hand on the back of her head. She breathed in and drew as much of it in as she could, sucking as it filled her mouth. As she perfected the act she began to enjoy it, pleased that she was the cause of his heightening excitement as the hand on the back of her head gripped her hair tighter and tighter. Eventually he stepped backwards and motioned for her to lean against the tree once more. He held her leg up and leaned against her, looking her full in the eyes. "Are you sure you want this?" he asked.

"Yes, yes," she said emphatically, and he guided himself in so quickly she gasped in surprise.

The tip of him softly and slowly stroked her insides. She gripped his shoulders tightly as he drew himself almost completely out before entering again. Placing her arms around his neck, she glimpsed the still frenzied licking and stroking by the campfire. Straining her eyes she thought she saw a figure loitering by the branches, but she couldn't be certain until he stepped slowly forward. He – she knew it was a he – leaned over the mass of bodies, his skin shining and movements dreamlike and strange. She watched him kneel down to Mary, whose tongue was servicing a girl lying on her back. Isabella watched the expression on Mary's face change. The sight of her leaning back in delighted abandon excited Isabella even more.

She watched the figure maneuver through the writhing women, finally settling near a resting Anne. Her blue eyes shone Indigo and she pulled the arm of Bessie, the girl nearest her, in an order to service her. Isabella felt the beginning of something stirring as she watched Bessie run a hand down Anne's pale, exposed side. Anne responded with a slight lift of her head and closed her eyes. Bessie lifted Anne's leg, entering her with her fingers as her thumb rolled across her stiff clitoris. A red flush swept over Anne's face as her eyes opened, aiming their gaze at Isabella. The stranger's thrusting against Isabella became more frantic until the sensation spread from her groin outwards, making her fingertips tingle and a rush flood her brain. She felt an overwhelming need to weep but instead she leaned forwards, her body becoming stiff. He looked down at her with a pleased expression, thrusting harder until he too moaned and grew still, resting his head next to hers against the tree.

She felt his weight shift from her and opened her eyes, a terrible exposure gripping her when she found herself alone, her dress rolled sausage-like around her middle. The heat of his breath and the heaviness of his body had deserted her as she pulled her clothes on straight and wiped away the liquid that ran down her leg with some leaves. A confused sob escaped her as she turned to the campfire but relief flooded her when she saw the sleeping mass of bodies. As she nestled against Mary, she could almost feel his fingertips again.

**

Through autumn Isabella returned to everyday life, privately awaiting the return of the stranger. As each day passed his fingertips and tongue faded, and Isabella began to wonder increasingly whether it had happened at all. Her husband Mark had noticed nothing unusual, but she felt her body change. The air grew colder, bringing increased worry and sadness.

Closing the gate behind the hens, she almost dropped the basket of seed when she saw him sitting on a tree stump. Excitedly she ran to him before stopping, appraising him with uncertainty.

"Forgive me for my absence," he said.

Isabella folded her arms and looked downwards.

"I have much to attend to, but I will come when I can," he continued, and Isabella felt her resolve slip under the same gaze that had looked at her so heatedly.

She stepped forwards, her arms still folded.

"You were lucky *I* came to you," he continued. "Legion came for the other women." Isabella frowned, unwilling to ask what he meant lest she seem foolish. He pulled her to him and when he embraced her she thought of nothing.

***

Isabella knelt on the ground while Mary shook the dried leaves over the small fire. "It will not light. The ground is wet," laughed Isabella.

"No, it shall." Mary continued to hold the tinder to the sticks with a determination Isabella had never seen in the frivolous girl.

"Surely we can wish for good crops at the usual time. Why must it be done now?" asked Isabella as the wind pushed her hair across her face. Mary ignored her as the sticks caught the flames. She placed her hands over them as protection.

"Isabella," she said sharply, "Take the leaves and scatter them." Isabella did as she was told, furrowing her brow when she heard the words the other girl spoke. Convinced she must be wrong, she followed her friend back through the trees. She almost mentioned the new life inside her, but the words didn't come.

For several weeks she thought no more of the incantation in the woods until a furious shouting pierced the open windows. She hurried outside to see the pig farmer, Atkin Foreman, arguing with his neighbor Simon Jansen.

Chiding herself for nosiness, she listened intently in the doorway. "Atkin, pigs fall ill. 'Tis the way of nature. Perhaps the cold air seeped under the barn door."

"Are you accusing me of leaving the door open and murdering my own animals?" Atkin bellowed.

"Of course not," spluttered Simon after a shocked silence, "but these things will happen, unfortunate as they are."

"I am telling you, there is sorcery afoot," snapped Atkin, "and your answer is to accuse *me*?"

"Well, Atkin," Simon appealed, "Why should someone wish to curse your livestock?" The farmer's mouth closed, his face turning an ugly plum. Without replying he stomped back to his fields, leaving his neighbor calling helplessly after him.

After the sun set Isabella's husband happily spooned hot pottage into his mouth. Isabella watched his gentle features, picturing his horror if he knew her secret activities. His face was trusting and he had always been so kind and, though she had occasionally felt a prickle of guilt after her forays into the woods, it was nothing compared to the desolate confusion she felt as she placed a hand over her growing bump. She knew it had to be done and she put her spoon down decisively. "We are expecting," she announced, unable to look at him directly. An inscrutable expression passed his face as he digested the news, but a moment later he was embracing her with joy. She let him hold her, wincing when he didn't complain about her wish to abstain that night.

When morning rose Isabella sought the mindless hustle of the town market. She breathed in strong spices carried by ships from far-off lands and aromatic herbs, and avoided the clumsy hooves of cattle, sheep and horses. Their sweat was strong and the scent of manure alerted the chattering crowds to the piles dotting the roads. Isabella's thoughts were comfortably drowned under the bargaining, calls to lost friends and fearful animal bellowing. She drifted to a stall guarded by an old woman selling ancient remedies of henbane and chamomile, her eyes shifting for any sign of Puritan officials. "Is it strong?" Isabella asked.

"Chamomile can be eaten, and the henbane is decorative," the old lady answered brusquely. When a nearby family passed to the next stall she nodded to Isabella. "Aye, strong it is. The henbane will vanish all pain from where it's rubbed and one infusion of the chamomile is enough to calm even the most anxious if mixed with enough Valerian." Isabella nodded and purchased a small amount, surreptitiously hiding the contents of her basket with her hand.

She intended to pass the crowds and make her way home when something stopped her. A husband and wife chatted blithely with a stallholder, a stout gentleman selling vegetables. "A rabbit appeared at our doorway, and since then Sarah has taken sick. We fear it may be the pox and all the while that thing lurked outside." The husband placed an arm around his distressed wife.

"'Tis true, some strange goings on and no mistake. The other day I spoke to the Millers in the tavern; three in their area have had children come down with the pox and Goodwife Didcott lost her baby altogether. Animals keep taking sick too, and a few houses have all but collapsed." He shook his head in confusion. "Strange goings on," he repeated, and his audience concurred.

With a stomach of mixed feelings Isabella made her way back through the woods. She had reconciled herself to never seeing the stranger again and at first she didn't recognize him. She felt the now familiar jolt of childish joy and trotted towards him.

He smiled but, as she let him embrace her, she knew the happiness would be short-lived. She told herself to live in the moment, studying his face when she pulled back. She wanted to ask him about the behavior of the others, and knew that she should, but she couldn't risk making him leave early.

"Your friends are heading for trouble," he muttered. Isabella nodded, thinking of Mary suffering at the hands of the frightened townsfolk. He kissed her on the forehead and she closed her eyes, but when she opened them he had gone.

***

Her belly grew big and with it, Mark's excitement. He prepared for the arrival of a child that wasn't his, unknowing of the nights she lay awake reliving her encounter in the woods. The spring sun brightened the sky and made the mud dusty, and Isabella took the opportunity to collect sweet-smelling herbs and flowers from the bushes near Atkin's farm. A bumblebee hummed around the blossoms and a wood pigeon sang tunelessly from the boughs of a tree, and it was with contentment that she picked the purple cone of an Echinacea plant. Placing it in her basket, she turned to leave when she heard a man's voice calling.

Confused, she looked up to see Simon Jansen tearing across the field towards her. "You know Mary, do you not?" he demanded as he shook her by the arms. Isabella struggled fearfully against his grip. "Tell me what she has done. Tell me how to undo it!" cried Simon.

When he saw the blank, frightened expression on her face he went limp. "The pox has taken his sight and his senses. He just tells Mary Samson he is sorry as if she is stood right there in the room watching him."

Isabella knew she should comfort him but panic made her double over. Simon watched dumbly before asking if he should call the midwife. She shook her head, trying to breathe evenly as she hobbled to Mary's home. She found her leaning over a wooden tub by the bushes, scrubbing the sheets clean against the washboard. Her reddened hands made a splash in the water when Isabella called out her name. "You arrived so silent I didn't hear you," she laughed nervously. Isabella couldn't return the smile.

"What has happened to Atkin Foreman and his livestock?" she asked sharply.

"What?" Mary stood up straight, her face flushing. "His livestock has met no mischief. If they have it is only because he is a drunk who doesn't take care of anything." Isabella paused, confusion and self-doubt draining her anger. "You didn't – you thought I cursed them in the woods that time?" the hurt on Mary's face was almost unbearable. Isabella's face lowered in shame.

"I cannot blame you," Mary continued, stepping closer. "I did cast a different spell in the woods that day." Alarm seeped back into Isabella and she felt her throat closing.

"I wanted to make Peter Goode notice me," grinned Mary. Isabella exhaled; her head was light from holding her breath. Embarrassment prickled her and she tried to apologize. "Think not of it," Mary replied, wiping her hands on her smock. "Oh, you have water on your boots."

"I shall clean them when I get home – it is only water," said Isabella dismissively, wanting to leave and forget the last hour. She was alarmed when, instead of wiping her boots and standing up again, Mary's hand snaked underneath the hem of Isabella's skirts. Mary's behavior in such a domestic setting was so unexpected that Isabella froze, unable or unwilling to move. She knew Mary's husband would be inside the house overlooking them, but Mary seemed not to have the same concerns. "I bet you Mark is afraid to touch you in your condition," muttered Mary. "If he knew what you had been up to?"

Isabella gritted her teeth against the tickle of Mary's fingers as they crept past her long underwear and towards her private lips. Despite her wish to save Mary from rash and hedonistic actions, she felt the wetness come as Mary's finger probed the entrance to her opening. Knowing that they could be caught, that Mary's husband might even see them now, Isabella still parted her legs. The back of her mind chided her, but the forefront breathed heavily as Mary's finger slid inside, her thumb circling the front of her mound. "I wanted you to notice me too," said Mary in a low voice, "I like to watch you come." Isabella considered pretending she had felt the release to get away faster when she felt the first stirrings. Her eyes looked down at Mary's, who smiled at the other's surprise.

Isabella gently rolled her hips with Mary's thumb as she chanced a glimpse at the window. As she moaned she spied Mary's husband drifting past, his eyes focused on something in the room. Isabella knew she should stop her friend but instead the shuddering coursed through her body, the rush of sensation and feeling. When reality began to settle she pulled away from the other girl, her eyes darting about the yard. "I have a lot to do," she explained vaguely, turning from the strange scene and walking as quickly as her bump allowed.

As the summer sun ripened, Isabella's anxiety festered. Each new day brought another tale of underhanded deeds and accusations, and all the while she struggled to maintain serenity.

As a particularly hot day cooled to evening, the pains began. She grabbed onto a chair, terror shooting through her body. She wailed for her husband, who ran to fetch the midwife and Isabella's female relatives. She was chided for not confining herself by the old Widow and assisted to the bedroom.

Her aunt and sisters crowded around, chattering happily. Isabella envied them their thoughts and conversation, free as it was of double meaning and the need to check their words. She wept for the pain and the situation she was bringing her children into. "Worry not, my dear," the Widow assured confidently. "You are young and strong."

The evening melted into darkness and the pain and worry was so terrible Isabella thought her heart would break. Her head was churning and she wept at the thought of spending the night with no change but, as she thought she couldn't take any more, the Widow leaned down and urged her to push.

"It is almost at an end," she exclaimed, and Isabella laughed uncontrollably as the relief broke over her. Her sisters and aunt offered noisy encouragement and, after another age, Isabella felt a boulder pass down through her.

"You have a son!" the midwife announced as she severed the chord and swaddled him in blankets before handing him to her cooing relatives. Isabella reached for him but was held in place by the midwife's hand. She wailed again in agony, confused and frightened.

"Am I dying?" she cried.

"No, my dear," smiled the Widow benevolently, "You have twins." The women squealed in restrained excitement, her aunt rocking the first born in her arms. The pain tore through Isabella again, and a long minute later her screaming second child came into the world.

"Is that all there is to it? I could do it all again with ease," Isabella laughed weakly. The women told her how well she had done, leaving her to sleep as her sons settled. Isabella watched the dust dancing in the fading light, waiting for the release of sleep that wouldn't come.

***

Her newborn sons were the size of four-month-olds and each person she passed commented on their health and size. Isabella had never felt such pride before. As she set a fire in the grate she was surprised by a knock at the door. When she answered the cocoon she had built around herself and her family was destroyed. "Is it not terrible I have not been to see them before now?" asked Mary as she strolled indoors. "Oh, look at them," she whispered over the sleeping forms in their wicker cribs. Isabella forced a smile, watching the other girl closely. "He would be so proud. Of course, I am certain he can see them wherever he is. Lucifer chose you to bear his sons."

"I know," Isabella agreed quickly, the reminder bringing bittersweet thoughts.

"He will come to us and set us free," Mary continued, and Isabella saw something in her eyes that made her back away, something not entirely sane.

"Lucifer wants us to destroy it all, Isabella," said Mary, "and you're not helping us. Why will you not help us?" Isabella struggled for an answer, her eyes searching for something nearby she could use to protect herself.

Mary stepped forward. "You must come to the forest tonight," she explained. "We shall call him and bring death and disease to all." The excitement sparkled in her eyes the way it had in happier times.

"I will come to the forest," Isabella soothed. "I will see you there. I promise, Mary." Mary studied Isabella's face for signs of deceit and, satisfied, made her way to the door.

"We shall be there at the usual time," she said as she opened the door, "and if I do not see you I will be very upset. We shall all be very upset." Eyes wide, she shut the door behind her as Isabella slumped to the floor, broken and defeated.

The familiar scent of bracken and undergrowth enveloped her with the newly cold air as she stumbled towards the sounds of voices. The trusting look on her aunt's face as she left the children in her care had pulled heavily at her heart, but she tried to remain determined. The crunching leaves alerted the distant group to her presence, bringing two young women running from the trees. "Isabella!" they called loudly, to resounding pleas for quiet from the others.

Isabella stepped into the clearing, the other women pleased at her arrival. Mary raised her hand in a gesture for her to sit nearby. As she did so, Isabella noticed the same maniacal look in the eyes of each of them. She slunk to the back, watching Anna take her place at the center. "The time has approached," she said clearly, "for us to complete our plans. Mabon has again arrived, and this time our pleas will be answered directly. The townsfolk will pay for their treatment of us, for we have collected every act of hate and carelessness, and we shall react with great retribution. Tonight they shall know what they have done." She raised her eyes to the sky, her smile unhinged as the crowd cheered hysterically. Isabella looked around her fearfully, knowing the townspeople heard.

The women danced wildly and tore at their clothes, their baskets of dried flowers and herbs knocked askew by flailing feet. They bumped into each other heavily, laughter and animal noises rising from deep inside them. As they stripped and began to embrace, Anne regarded Isabella with dilated pupils. "I know you have wished to touch my skin," she said in a low voice. Isabella's throat tightened, her fingers closing around the tincture in her basket. Anne didn't notice; her purpose fixed entirely on Isabella. She ran her hands over Isabella's breasts. Isabella was tempted for a moment to let it happen as her nipple was teased by the other girl, as her body began to respond. She watched almost helplessly as Anne pulled at her dress, freeing her breast and sucking at its tip.

Gritting her teeth, Isabella began muttering.

"What is that you are saying?" asked Anne as she looked up. Isabella ignored her and continued, secretly prising the lid from the jar as Anne's lips drew charges of pleasure from deep within her.

Isabella closed her eyes as she whispered the last of her incantation, flinging the contents of the jar over the earth as Anne's tongue made her moan. Anne pulled away from her furiously, and the revelry of the other witches ceased with eerie suddenness.

"What have–" Anne's sentence was never finished as the clearing was filled with a violent roar.

Bodies of men flung themselves over prostate women, pulling them up and restraining them. Some wailed as they were dragged across the ground by their hair.

Isabella rose, struggling to cover herself. Sneaking towards the undergrowth, she was stopped by a thing made of iron.

Turning, she saw her husband gripping her wrist; his wounded expression grew cold and determined as he forced her to join the rest in being tied like hogs, and carted away to the prison.

The cell was dark and the stink of urine and sweat was palpable. Isabella wrapped herself in a ball amongst the straw, assaulted by the screams and pleas of her cellmates. The prison guards responded only by slamming their wooden sticks against the tiny barred window, their diseased lips parting to reveal brown teeth. "You belong here, you witches!" they called. "Your master cannot help you now. Once your trial is done you will hang, every last one of you. It is no more than you cockroaches deserve." Isabella knew they were right, and the hours stretched into days. She knew their master had seen the attention the others had drawn and abandoned them, also giving up on their children. She wondered if he had fathered more by other women and if he visited them often. She could no longer feel his gaze on her, and felt alone for the first time in a year.

The difference between day and night disappeared and the prisoners slept as often as they could. Isabella lay awake amongst the slumbering bodies, the straw scratching her skin and the ground hard and cold. She heard the distant conversation between the prison guards and placed her hands over her ears to silence them. A hand covered hers and she was at once wide awake, filled with adrenaline. It was the stranger, and she gripped him and wept. "Please keep them safe," she sobbed, "my boys have done nothing wrong." He stroked her hair until she was spent.

"No harm will come to them," he assured. Her heart filled with relief and, when he lay her back down onto the straw, she let sleep come.

CHAPTER 1

2007
OCTOBER 28 – 10 P.M.

It had been a grueling weeklong trek back and forth along the Ohio and Pennsylvania turnpikes behind the wheel of an eighteen-wheeler semi truck and Jonathan Harker was truly fatigued. *No man knows until he has suffered the long stretches of Pennsylvania's road construction how nice a comfortable bed and a warm, willing woman can be,* Jonathan thought to himself as he grinned.

The trucking company he was working for didn't leave him much of a social life, but it paid the bills. *As long as the steel mills stay open and the machine shops keep their orders coming in, I'll keep driving this rig 'til it kills me.*

Jonathan winced and rubbed his neck. His back and neck were killing him. Many years ago, he had been injured in an accident and although technically "healed," he still ached, especially on long hauls. Tonight was one of those "aching" nights.

Jonathan glanced at the clock on the dash and wondered if the Brown Derby would still be open. *I could go for a full rack of ribs and a cold glass of iced tea!* He pulled the truck off of Ohio Exit 234 and onto Interstate 690. He still had just over two hours to go to reach Sandusky, but in truth, he didn't have to be there until 6:00 a.m.

He reached into the rig's console and began looking around for some Advil. He found the bottle, but as he shook it, it was empty. *Damn!* Almost as if something psychological was added to his torment, his head began to throb near his temples.

Jonathan made his way past Youngstown and onto Ohio Route 422. The Brown Derby was tucked into the Niles/Warren area. As he approached the restaurant, it was lit up. *Probably should go and find a drug store first,* he thought; his neck was feeling tighter and tighter by the minute. He drove past the Brown Derby and began looking on both sides of the road for something that might be open. He pulled into a gas station hoping to get some pain relievers and get back to the Derby, but it was closed. Odd. He drove a little further. *Fuck it!* he thought, *I'll eat first and maybe the neck ache will go away.*

He pulled the rig into what he thought was a bank parking lot in order to turn the truck around. Oddly, it wasn't a bank but rather a spa of some sort. A brightly lit sign announcing *Lunar Radiance Spa* shined into his windshield. Next to the door, an LED "OPEN" sign was lit up.

Hot damn! Jonathan thought to himself. *A deep-tissue massage might be just the thing I need to get rid of this muscle tension.* He parked the truck in the rear of the establishment, got out, and walked back to the front. He reached for the door and found it was locked.

A wave of sheer disappointment washed over him and the cold Northeast Ohio night chilled him to the soul. Above the doorknob was a doorbell. He pressed it and waited.

When no one came to answer, he assumed the establishment was closed and began to walk away. He made it about ten steps when the door opened up behind him. An older oriental lady stood in the doorframe. She waved at Jonathan to come in.

"Hello!" Jonathan said as he approached.

"Hello," she replied in friendly return. "Please come in." The woman appeared to be in her fifties, with short dark hair, and stood roughly five feet in height. She reached for Jonathan's hand, and led him through the door. "It's very cold out there."

"I thought for a moment you were closed," Jonathan said.

"No. We're open. Please, come this way." She led Jonathan into a beautifully decorated treatment room. A twin bed with clean, white towels lay across it. In one corner of the room, a towel steamer was glowing. On the other side, a radio was playing. Oddly, it wasn't playing music, but rather a talk show. Two guys were having a discussion on weight loss or something. On the walls were mirrors that ran the entire length of the wall.

"I've been on the road all day long and my back, neck, shoulders – you name it – are really killing me." Jonathan told the woman, whom he thought was the masseuse.

"Are you from the area?" the lady asked.

Jonathan shook his head no. "Actually, I'm from West Virginia. Originally from a small town called Melas, but now I hang my hat in Wheeling. I travel a lot between here and northern Ohio. I make deliveries of specialized steel parts to various manufacturing plants in the region. I'm a bit road-weary and found you by accident." Jonathan looked a bit embarrassed and added, "I'm not coming in too late am I?"

The older lady grinned, "Not at all."

"How much for your massage treatments?"

"Fifty dollars for one hour, plus a tip for the therapist if you like."

"Let me check what I have," Jonathan said as he reached for his wallet. His heart raced because this was a spur-of-the-moment thing and he wasn't really sure how much he had on him. *Let's hope they take credit cards,* his mind countered. Ah, but he was in luck! He had roughly $140.00 in cash on him with a crisp fifty-dollar-bill in front. He grinned at the stern portrait of Ulysses S. Grant staring up at him from the wallet. He pulled the bill out and handed it to the lady. "I think we're in luck!"

"Very good!" the lady replied. "Your therapist will be in shortly."

About thirty seconds later a six-foot-tall Asian goddess walked in the room. *Holy fucking shit!* Jonathan thought as she bopped into the room with a cheery smile and happy wave. Unlike the shorter Asian woman he had just spoken with, this lady was what Jonathan's dad would refer to as "one long, tall drink of water."

She was remarkably sexy and stood before Jonathan wearing nothing but a peach-colored bikini. She appeared to be about twenty-five-years-old or thereabouts. Her hair was shoulder-length. Her breasts looked to be a C-cup and she didn't have one ounce of fat on her body. It was without exaggeration that she could have easily been a model for Victoria's Secret or some men's stroke magazine.

"Hello!" she said with a heavy accent.

"Hello." He reached out his hand in greeting. "My name is Johnny." Jonathan noticed the sound of his heartbeat in his ears as his pulse started racing.

She shook it. "I'm Tina." She gestured for him to talk off his coat. He did and handed it to her. She hung it on a clothes rack that he hadn't noticed upon his first inspection of the room.

"And your shirt, please." Tina said.

A rogue thought crossed Jonathan's mind: *She's not leaving the room, is she? Nope, she's not.*

Jonathan unbuttoned the long-sleeve black shirt he was wearing, glancing down at the company logo as he took it from his body and passed it to the therapist. He reflexively sucked in his gut in front of the beautiful lady.

"Pants too," Tina said with a nervous giggle in her voice, picking up on Jonathan's embarrassment, but not offering to leave the room.

Jonathan carefully kicked off his tennis shoes and socks, then proceeded to unbuckle his blue jeans and slide them to the floor. Now he was wearing only his boxers. He swiftly picked up the jeans from the floor and handed them to the woman.

Tina nicely straightened out the wad of pants and hung them professionally next to his shirt on the rack.

Jonathan proceeded to get on the bed but Tina stopped him. "Those too."

Jonathan blushed and obediently removed the boxer shorts.

"Now you can get on the bed." Tina said. "Face down."

For the next twenty minutes or so, Tina worked on Jonathan's back. It was truly one of the best massages he had ever had. The tension headache was miles away. She also worked on his butt – something he had never had done before – and being that he sat behind the wheel all day, he couldn't articulate how wonderful that felt.

She worked her way up to his arms, stretching them and inadvertently making his knuckles crack. He sighed in pleasure.

"You like?" she asked.

"Very much so," he replied. "You're amazing."

Unlike any masseuse he ever had in the past, she bent down and kissed him on the cheek. He turned on his side and looked up at her dark eyes. They held such mystery. There was almost a magical quality about her that he couldn't quite put his finger on, but *something* was definitely different about Tina.

"Would you like an extra massage?" she asked.

He was not sure what exactly she meant by that, but something in his very being just *knew* that the relief he just experienced on his back was only the beginning of greater pleasures ahead, should he answer this question affirmatively.

"Absolutely."

She got off the bed and went over to where his pants were hanging. She reached in and handed Jonathan his wallet.

He flashed through the remaining currency: four twenties and one ten. "How much?" he asked.

She smiled and shrugged.

"Ninety dollars is everything in my wallet," Jonathan said.

She came closer and whispered. "If you want *everything,* that will be one-fifty."

"I'm sorry," Jonathan said as he pulled out the money. "All I have is ninety. See." He fanned the empty billfold for her to see that he wasn't trying to bluff her, that he only had ninety. Truth be told, Tina was most definitely worth one-fifty, but Jonathan would just have to see where this was going to lead.

She grinned and winked. "Let me see." She counted the five bills that Jonathan had in his hand: "Two, four, six, eight, nine. I'll be right back." Tina took the money and disappeared, closing the door behind her.

For the next five minutes, Jonathan stared up at the ceiling, wondering if he was doing the right thing. *Probably too late for that old chap,* his mind thought. *Maybe she's calling the cops on you!* another part of his brain replied.

Jonathan – now on his back – simply stared up at the tiled ceiling and waited. The radio was still going on: "*... and studies show that those who lost weight would gain it back once they returned to their old diets. I don't know about you, but I don't need a scientific study to know that if I reduced calories and lost weight, and then returned to my old eating habits, the weight would come back...*"

The goddess was back, somehow more radiant than before, and grinning from ear-to-ear.

In actuality, Jonathan would have gladly settled for an ongoing repeat of the back rub. However, he was about to experience a whole lot more.

Tina placed something underneath Jonathan's pillow and kissed him on the neck. He felt the hairs on his chest stand up. She was electrifying!

Tina moved off the bed, unfastened her bikini top, and laid it on a nearby chair. A perfect set of C-cups with dark brown nipples spilled out before a nervous Jonathan.

She also slipped off her bottom and began caressing his thighs, ankles, and feet. She began performing the most amazing foot massage and for a moment, Jonathan drifted off into a relaxing slumber.

Almost as if sensing that Jonathan was becoming more relaxed than aroused, Tina quickly moved to remedy the situation, moving up to his groin, then up to his chest, then to his face. She gave him another kiss, "You like?"

He stared up at her, into those dark, mysterious eyes and replied: "Most definitely."

She resumed caressing him all over and he couldn't help but feel himself harden at the stimulation. Tina came back up to kiss him some more, reaching for his manhood and bringing it to full erection.

She reached underneath the pillow to retrieve the item she had placed there earlier: a condom.

The couple lay on the bed facing each other. Tina began kissing Jonathan's neck and Jonathan did likewise to Tina's. Her dark hair brushed his face and her dark eyes sparkled in the dim light of the room. Through their exchange of erogenous zone stimulation, Jonathan felt Tina place the condom on his very erect penis and guide it into her tastefully trimmed pubic mound.

She let out a sigh as the two bonded in sexual intercourse on their sides. Jonathan never really "did it" on the side before, but this experience was unique and exhilarating. As he caressed her soft, slender butt as her hips pumped in rhythm with his, he felt newly formed beads of sweat forming on her back as she became more and more aroused.

Tina grabbed his hands in hers and pressed him to the bed, moving from the side position to a comfortable "woman-on-top" position. Tina was a sexpot of Asian passion and seeing her so excited and in control made Jonathan's love muscle flex even more. She let out a wail in delight.

Jonathan glanced over at the mirror to take in the image of both of their bodies in passionate harmony. That's when he noticed something very strange...

In the mirror, Tina appeared to have an outline of wings. They were very faint, almost ghost-like. Her body was surrounded by a light-blue aura that radiated downward onto his.

Tina caught Jonathan's eyes looking at the mirror and looked that way herself.

She blushed; he had seen it!

To cover it up and distract Jonathan, she passionately called out, "Switch sides!"

Tina flung herself on the bed and guided Jonathan to missionary on top of her. Jonathan pumped her in this position for about five minutes before collapsing on top of her in a mind-blowing orgasm.

Tina quickly got up and grabbed some steamed towels from the small appliance in the room and began cleaning Jonathan; removing the condom and wiping his groin area in loving caresses.

"You looked like you had wings," Jonathan said.

Tina put her index finger to her lips to indicate for him to be quiet. She sat down next to him, put her arm around his neck, and giggled nervously, "You see?"

Jonathan could tell that her English was not very good, but had understood completely that her non-verbal skills more than made up for that. He nodded affirmatively.

"No tell, okay?" Tina requested, a hint of concern in her eyes.

"What are you?" Jonathan whispered.

Tina bent in and kissed him on the lips, "Let's get dressed."

She dutifully helped Jonathan get his clothes on, even putting his socks on for him and lacing up his shoes. Jonathan was spellbound and had never had such loving treatment from a woman in his entire life. As he left the room, the older Asian lady was in the establishment's front area waiting for the couple to come out.

Tina spoke something in what Jonathan believed to be Japanese to the elder and for a brief moment the two ladies exchange glances and rapid conversation. The older woman smiled and reached for Jonathan's hand, guiding him to a set of couches in the front room.

"You are glowing!" she exclaimed. "You seem much more relaxed and happy!"

"What can I say," Jonathan agreed. "I feel wonderful!"

"Tina seems pretty happy too!" the lady said, laughing. She knew the two had just finished having unbelievably good sex but didn't seem to mind.

"We hope to see you back real soon. I know Tina would like that. She fancies you."

"I really had a good time, but I did have a question..."

"No questions. Okay."

Jonathan shrugged.

"I will tell you something, but you must promise to please keep what I am about to tell you to yourself."

"I can do that." Jonathan said.

"We are an ancient race of magical beings. Most humans cannot detect us as being different from them. Only spirits tied to a greater destiny can see our true form. Typically, our magic is good enough to conceal ourselves, but the way that you loved Tina back there broke her spell. She let her guard down and revealed her true form."

The older lady pondered for a moment thinking about her next words. "Tina. She is a – oh, how to you say it in English? A *tenshi*."

Jonathan stared at her blankly, not understanding her.

"Umm," the older lady continued, looking for some other word that could she could use to help the stranger understand. "She is a *fae* and so am I. Please do not tell others, as they will hunt us down. We are an endangered race."

"You need not worry, madam. I will keep this experience to myself."

"Thank you very much."

The older woman walked Jonathan to the door and he turned and waved goodbye to her and Tina. The young masseuse blushed and giggled, waving back.

The brisk, late-October air in Northeast Ohio was chilly and wet. Jonathan left the Lunar Radiance Spa renewed and relaxed. Getting back into his truck, he drove away toward Sandusky, completely forgetting about catching something to eat at the Brown Derby.

Jonathan pulled the rig into a rest area just before his exit to sleep the four hours or so before he had to be at work. He would wake up and write off the "magic" he saw as something his tired mind had dreamed up.

In the weeks, months, and years to follow, the unique experience would fade into the recesses of Jonathan's psyche like a lucid dream that one tucks away in those private places, to think about on dark nights when one needs to remember what living is all about. However faded the "dream" would become, it was not completely forgotten.

CHAPTER 2

12 September –

Note to self: get the hell out of West Virginia. This state has some fucked up laws! My bastard of a stepfather, Monte, just dropped me off at the Loony Bin! Self-righteous son-of-a-bitch! I cannot believe this! They think I'm a sex addict! What the FUCK!?

He seemed almost delighted on the way up to Weston – told me that in THIS state, a man can simply drop a woman off at Weston if he suspects she has a mental disease. They'll even give him a reward! Mental disease my ass! I was playing with myself (although I do admit that it was in church, but that's beside the point!). How was I to know that he and Deacon Jones would barge in like some lynch mob? Church was in session and I was over at the activity building. Wasn't Monte supposed to be preaching or something?

FUCK! I'm so screwed now. They just checked me in and I'm stuck in this orange-walled room, waiting for someone to "examine" me. I'm very pissed off, but I am COMPLETELY in my right mind. Gotta go.

***

Ok. I just spent four hours dealing with nurses, social workers, and one really weird-looking dude who just happened to pop into the room and tell me about how he liked to draw beaver cats. I'm thinking to myself, "That guy's not getting anywhere near my beaver!" Luckily the nurse came in and escorted the young perv away before he whipped out the old pen and pad – or some other "tool"!

Hopefully I won't be here too long. The social worker thought that maybe Monte overreacted (no surprises there) and that as soon as a full "psycho" evaluation has been performed he is confident that I can get out of here in no time. I still have to stay the night, so we'll see how this goes...

13 September –

My God, this place is creepy! It's four floors of madness – and the screaming! Holy SHIT! I'm thinking that if you're not crazy when you come in, you're going to be crazy when you leave! That was the longest night ever! How I prayed for the dawn. I didn't sleep a bit. The doctor never came. I spent the entire night scared shitless listening to the screams.

***

Just came back from breakfast, yes, with the rest of the nutcases. Everybody's eating like one big happy family in the cafeteria. Well, maybe not EVERYBODY, as I passed several people on gurneys as I walked to the mess hall. Very strange, the folks on the gurneys were all wearing sunglasses with patches over their eyes. Must be doing Lasik here or something.

Nurse Maddie came by the room and asked how I was doing. What do you think I told her?

"Just fine Maddie, this place is like a resort!" I don't think she liked my joke.

She said that I looked a little pale. Given the fact that I hadn't slept at all last night, it all comes with the territory. Anyway, maybe today I'll get to meet the doctor and get the hell out of here.

***

Let me get this out before I puke. Wanting the doctor to pay me a visit may not have been a good thing. He called himself Henry, but I swear that guy looked like that Nazi dude for those old war movies – Himmler or something.

Anyway, Henry took me to a room on the second floor and said that he needed to perform a physical on me. This was very odd, because, after all, wasn't I here for my MIND? Hello, people! Physically, I'm fine. I told him that. He just grinned at me behind his round, wire-rimmed glasses and proceeded to tell me to take off my clothes – that perv!

I resisted at first. Boy was that a mistake! He left the room and came back with two male nurses. One of them was carrying a syringe with a huge-ass needle.

"Miss Davenport," Henry said in a thick German accent, "you should really consider cooperating. Now – take off your clothes!"

Yeah, I guess I overreacted; I punched one of the motherfuckers in the nose. He let out a yelp, but not before the second one stuck me with the syringe.

I blacked out. The next thing I knew I was completely naked and shackled. The room was not much bigger than a closet and on the left and right walls were two hooks – one at the foot-level and another about three feet above it. Both of my feet were manacled and chained to the bottom hooks and my arms were chained to the top ones; left and right respectively.

I couldn't sit down; the chains kept me from that. I just stood there in my birthday suit and waited. I don't really know how long I was out, but when I woke up, Henry was there. He positively frightened me! His eyes were so intense!

"Are you ready to cooperate now, Miss Davenport?" he asked. I nodded. "Very good."

I remember him licking his lips and saying in a heavy German accent: "If you cooperate, your stay here will be an endurable one. If you don't... well then, maybe not so much."

CHAPTER 3

September 13 -

The new patient – a young female: Amanda Davenport – is the perfect subject for my very particular and experimental approach. I tire of performing transorbital lobotomies, although I much prefer the physicality of thrusting a leucotome ice pick through the eye socket than the dull prescription of anti-psychotic drugs. People say that lobotomies are outmoded, but they have served me well since the 1940's. I have always been exceedingly fascinated by physical procedures. The effects of intervention upon the body... mmm... excites me, it would be true to confess.

You might say that I am very much a "hands-on" psychiatrist.

You can well imagine my delight when my nursing staff informed me that an alleged female "sex addict" had been admitted and registered for treatment under our very capable care.

It is most fortuitous that the young woman naturally presents certain psychological symptoms that befit my purposes most ideally. Miss Davenport's overt use of swear-words and her adolescent rantings belie her manifestation of classic sexual addiction. Sex addiction is not currently in the DSM, the *Diagnostic and Statistical Manual of Mental Disorders*, but I intend to ensure that I have sufficient empirical evidence to prove that it merits a place there. I hunger for recognition from my peers as much as I hunger for...

But enough. Suffice to say, I have my own personal reasons for conducting a little personal research, shall we say.

Miss Davenport was barely enthusiastic at the prospect of incarceration in this institution. Her language was most unseemly for a lady. Which, clearly, she is not. I warned her that cooperation would be most efficacious to her good health and recovery, and I am certain that she will acquiesce since she has no choice in the matter. If pure physical restraint does not prevail (and she did most brutally attack a nurse), we can always resort to drugs.

I started by breaking down her barriers in my usual way. Some people may call the process "flooding," but I have a more refined approach. Certainly it is my goal to take her own exhibitionist tendencies outside of her personal control, and to the limit. So if she is bound naked and spread-eagled, her natural vulnerability should overwhelm her own desire to expose herself in a sexual manner in public. It all makes perfect sense.

My simple definition of the term "sexual addiction" is the behavior of a person who has an unusually intense sex drive or an obsession with sex. Sex and the constant thought of sex dominate the sex addict's thinking, so they cannot undertake normal work or engage in normal personal relationships.

Sex addicts like Miss Davenport display distorted thinking, rationalizing and justifying their behavior and blaming others rather than themselves. Characteristically, she is in denial about the problem and proclaims excuses for her abnormal actions. I questioned her about the range of activities she engaged in, analyzing her risk-taking sexual activity in the face of dangerous consequences, such as exhibitionism, stranger sex, obscene phone calls, and molestation. Symptoms include compulsive masturbation, multiple affairs, multiple or anonymous sexual partners and one-night stands, pornography, unsafe sex, cybersex, prostitution, obsessive dating, voyeurism, stalking, and sexual harassment.

When asked which of the activities she engaged in, Miss Davenport answered in the affirmative to all of them.

"Doesn't everyone?" she responded.

"No," I replied. "You are a very special person."

September 15 -

The physical procedures I have undertaken with Miss Davenport have proved most satisfactory. I must say with some delight that she "appears to be responding to treatment." That's what I tell her family, and it amuses me very much that I can tell her concerned relatives that fact, in all honesty, with all the pomposity and gravity of a consultant psychiatrist; and at the same time delight in my experiences of just how "responsive" she is to my "physical treatments."

I am very pleased with her progress. Every phrase with which I describe her case becomes filled with sexual innuendo. A metaphor for her psychological state!

It would be a fascinating study to find that sexual addiction is contagious, and that I, as her physician, have been contaminated by her disease. I can assure everyone, however, that this is not the case. Neither is it a case of transference, the attribution of feelings towards the subject from the therapist. I would need to feel emotions, and to have feelings, for that to be the case. This simply does not compute.

She is nothing but a guinea-pig. Less than being the subject of my experiments, this woman is simply the object. Human lives are expendable, and if they are expended in the service of my acquisition of knowledge, my furthering of my career, this is acceptable. Better still if lives are expended to fulfill my physical desires, my lust in experiencing bodily responses. This particular "object" and this particular experiment satiates my intellectual and physical curiosities.

It is such a shame that I cannot explore death with too many patients. More than two or three per year within this hospital is likely to raise suspicion. Even then, unless they are old, it raises questions. And who wants to experiment on wrinkled old bodies? Give me firm young flesh every time. If it means that I can continue with younger people in this vein (haha – that pun would amuse my Master), then I am happy to experiment to the edge of death and consciousness. Although with this woman, it would be most delicious to go beyond.

September 17 -

Following the success of physical interventions (very enjoyable to me), I have initiated psychological unconsciousness intrusion procedures, in which I visit her while she is sleeping or in a dream-state. Again, I have found these particular interventions to be highly successful. They certainly meet my needs to explore the psychology of terror.

The advantage of this technique is that I can inflict any kind of emotional and physical effect upon the object, and the object survives. I am exploring negative emotions in the extreme: horror, terror, pain, and using the object's imagination to provide the physicality of the experience.

For example, while Miss Davenport sleeps, I visit her in the form of a rabid wolf-beast. I hunt her down at length, and eventually fall upon her and ravish her. And *ravage* her, in fact. I can rip her flesh apart with my jagged teeth; literally tear her limb from limb. And the beauty of it is, I can do the same again, every single night! Except that would be tedious and repetitious. Even better is the fact that I can terrorize her in whatever form I choose, tapping into her deepest fears, and still she will survive to awaken the next morning.

It will be particularly noteworthy work when I integrate both the real, physical torment within the treatment room, simultaneously with the psychological unconsciousness intrusion. This means that while she sleeps, I will apply both real-time physical "torture" and intrude into her dreams to apply psychological pain and dream pain. I know that this has never been done before, and there is a risk of the object's death, but it is too significant a piece of investigation to resist. It is worth any risk!

But first, I must gather enough information from her dreams and unconscious fears to equip me to make the integrated process fully operable. That is, when I conduct the dual physical – psychological, conscious – unconscious, reality – dream experiment, I will know enough of her fear and pain thresholds to make the results cataclysmic.

September 22 -

O, what unanticipated horror! Tonight I was prepared for the ultimate experiment, and just when I had attached electrodes to Davenport's erogenous zones, and induced a dream-state through the careful administration of a mild sedative, I made the intrusion into her unconsciousness.

I took the form of a huge spider, with black furry legs as thick as tree trunks. Knowing that her arachnophobia was coupled with a fear of being attacked by a masked mugger, I ensured that the grotesque oversized body had a faceless human head attached, and began my scuttling, hairy march towards Davenport through a narrow alleyway, where her exit was blocked by a large electrified gate. She was screaming, and at the highest pitch of her dream fear, I decided to switch on the current through the real electrodes to give her a "double-whammy" of pain and terror within both dream and reality.

For a moment, I truly believed that dream had transcended reality. As the dream-Davenport cowered, shivering near the humming electrified gate, I flicked the switch that would shock the real Davenport strapped to the examination couch in my treatment room.

There was a blue flash, which alarmed me most distractingly. I lost concentration and broke the link into the woman's dream, but it was too late. I saw that the dual intervention had activated something primeval and deeply hidden in the woman. She glowed with a light-blue light surrounding her entire body, and behind her there had appeared a huge pair of opalescent wings, trembling like a dragonfly. Although not in fear. In *strength*.

I hissed loudly and stepped back, recoiling at the sight. A FAE! How could this be? It had been centuries past when the fae had been at war with the vampires and both sides were nearly destroyed. As far as we knew, the fae *were* completely destroyed! That was my firm belief until I saw Davenport's fae spirit flex when she was under experimentation.

How had I not perceived this long before? I could only conclude that she must be part human and part fae, a mongrel creature, an amalgamation of my two most despised species.

My instinct was to kill her immediately. The only thing that stopped me was my experience at Toad Road Asylum.

I wasn't keen to repeat *that* ordeal, and to lose my captives here. It is such an upheaval having to find new premises and patients. It's bad enough when I have to pretend to age and move on before people realize that I change little during the average human life cycle. I was concerned that if I killed Davenport here in the hospital, that she might burn up the entire place upon her passing.

For, she surely was a fae, whether she knew it or not.

Yet, she could not be aware of this genetic anomaly within her structure, or else she would have attacked me earlier. What a lucky escape for me!

It's even worse when the fae recognizes a cambion and intends to kill them! Some of the fae know how to defeat cambions with a lethal form of fae high magic – either by fire when they die, or when a fae bands together with at least one other to defeat a common enemy.

If both myself and my brother Talman can be killed in the same day, we meet "true death." If Davenport learns this – or more importantly, learns how to channel her magic – she could defeat both of us with her hidden powers. But first she'd have to realize this, and secondly, find another fae. Highly unlikely. Or die in my presence. She was more likely to do that here than anywhere else in the world.

I am declaring her cured and will immediately discharge her tomorrow!

CHAPTER 4

Mick Goldbloom looked over at his friend at the auto dealer in Phoenix. "Jay, the price is absurd, but it is a very nice ride."

Jay Christiano was grinning from ear to ear as he opened the driver's side door to the brand new Ford Shelby Mustang GT500 he had just purchased. He inhaled deeply, "Ah, gotta love a new car smell."

Mick simply stood watching as his friend climbed in and closed the door. The car did look impressive from the outside – its performance white paint job with black sports striping and dark wheels looked ready to take on anything on the road. Jay seemed to tune in on his friend's thoughts and added, "I'll be blazing my way through town on a white horse!" he said with excitement.

"Um, you mean like 550 horses," Mick replied as he stood suspiciously with arms crossed. "A nice, young Jewish man such as you should be settling down and getting married, not spending all his money on a fancy muscle car."

Jay laughed. "If I listened to you, I would be out shopping for minivans! Just face it, you're jealous that *you're* driving the family mobile and I get to cruise around in this fine ride."

This time, Mick laughed with his friend, "Busted."

"So, you'll be okay running things while I'm gone?" Jay asked. The two worked together at Mamlakah Construction and were fairly successful real estate investors. They had just completed a large housing project and Jay was taking some time off for vacation and to play with his new "toy."

"Sure," Mick affirmed. "Go off and have your fun. I'll be here slaving away."

"Take care old friend," Jay said as he started up the Shelby.

"Old friend, you say?" Mick scoffed. "You're making me sound like I'm ready for Social Security!"

"Well, you are driving a mini-van." Jay pulled away from the dealer lot.

"Youth!" Mick muttered to himself, shaking his head, as he returned to his vehicle.

He couldn't begrudge Jay his new car. After all, Jay was the nicest guy he knew. Too good to be true at times, but not in a nerdy way. He was handsome, hardworking, clean living, funny. A great guy – with a brand new, top-of-the-line, customized Ford Shelby Mustang GT500 convertible.

In fact, I should hate him! Mick thought, with a sardonic smile.

He pulled open the door and turned the key. His engine coughed, and he shook his head in disbelief, trying again, before it spluttered into life. On this occasion, he was glad to eat Jay's dust, watching his smooth white ride glide away before him. He was mortified to think Jay might have witnessed his embarrassment. Again. Much as he loved the guy, Mick didn't want to give Jay the satisfaction of that. Again.

***

Delighted, like a kid with a new toy, Jay didn't even look back through the rear-view mirror. He had worked hard for this treat and he was going to enjoy it to the max. He sped through town, grinning like a loon, hoping to see someone he knew so he could hail them and draw attention to his Mustang, his white teeth gleaming against his light growth of black beard. He turned every dial, pressed every button, pulled every lever, pressed the car horn, wiped the windshield, sprayed the windshield, wiped the windshield again, and accidentally popped open the trunk, mid-drive.

Laughing, he didn't even mind pulling over to the curb, just for the joy of it. He climbed out and opened the trunk fully, marveling at its immaculate black interior.

"Look. Isn't that gorgeous?" he said openly, showing the inside of his trunk with an expansive hand to a passing woman, who only frowned.

She looked at him as if he was a serial killer trying to entice her into his trunk, and hurried on.

He caressed the sleek flank of his white mustang and sighed, "I think I'm in love with you, White Horse!"

***

Jay had folded down the Mustang convertible's black roof and was enjoying the gentle breeze that caught his longish black wavy hair. He held his left hand out of the car to feel the soft wind of the cool air, letting it rush between his tanned fingers.

Whoa, Mama! This car was worth its money already, he thought to himself. The otherwise silent engine merely purring even at seventy miles per hour; the luxury of the soft leather interior and comfortable seat that fit him like a glove.

He had lived a selfless and modest life to date, starting off helping his dad in the carpentry business, then progressing via construction to realty. Things were just getting good in life, his career picking up and he had a great circle of friends. This automobile was his first real indulgence in his life, and he would turn thirty-three in four days. So Jay reckoned he deserved a little luxury now that things were on the up.

Most of his work lately had been real estate development in Phoenix – a very hot, desert climate.

Originally from the small town of Bethlehem, Pennsylvania, close to the state's beloved Pocono mountains and ski resorts, Jay was an overheated north-easterner longing for cooler weather. For his birthday he decided to go on vacation somewhere completely different, and planned a skiing trip to West Virginia. He booked a week's stay at Canaan Valley Ski Resort in Davis, bought his new Mustang, and was ready to go.

His friend and business partner, Mick, of course had called him crazy.

"Buying a brand new muscle car – even if mid-life crisis hadn't hit yet – was okay," he relented, grudgingly.

"If you could afford it and had no wife to nag you or kids to put through college, then do it." Mick had both, and couldn't. And taking a vacation was fine too. "Sure – do it!" he had told him.

But when Jay had announced that he would be driving 1,800 miles cross country in a premium vehicle that did only twenty-three miles per gallon on the highway – now that was plain stupid, in Mick's book.

"Any normal person would fly!" Mick had rolled his eyes on hearing Jay's plans.

"If God had meant us to fly, he'd have given us wings!" Jay had retorted, unwilling to listen to reason.

"Train, bus…" continued Mick, practical as ever.

Jay raised an eyebrow, "I like to be in charge of my own destiny. This way, I can enjoy my car, and stop wherever I like, whenever I like. Oh, freedom!" he grinned, his voice rising tunefully, "Freedom!"

"Please spare me the Aretha Franklin…" groaned Mick.

"Free-ee-do-o-om!" Jay danced off, jazz hands waving.

Jay just didn't like flying in planes and anyway, he would enjoy driving the 1,800-odd miles to West Virginia, seeing the country as he traveled. He enjoyed meeting people, trying new things, and this was a great opportunity to chill out, please himself, and get away from it all.

Boy, did Jay need this vacation! It felt like he hadn't slept properly for weeks, and it wasn't even as if he had things on his mind. Work was going great – their latest big property deal had gone smoothly and sweet as a nut. And he had no worries in the world.

So why were his nights broken by the same nightmare scenarios?

It started with one. Several months went by, then another. They became more violent and more frequent. Now, he was having them every night and had almost reached a breaking point with his insomnia.

His first nightmare happened three years ago and even to this day, Jay could remember it as if it were yesterday. He found himself on a desolate country road in the middle of a chilly night walking up to a clearing. Ahead of him was a dimly lit utilitarian-style brick building set up on a small knoll.

It was some type of school; a high school maybe? Jay didn't know, but in the dream he was compelled to place one foot in front of the other and inch his way closer to the oppressive structure. Almost like climbing the stairs of a Mayan pyramid, Jay climbed the stairs to the school and opened the front door.

A gripping doom grabbed his psyche and held on like a pit bull. He passed dozens of lockers as he walked to the rear hallway. He turned a corner and saw an overweight security guard and a ruffled man in a thrown-together suit walking in the same direction as he was just a few paces ahead.

"Care to show me where you found Jo Lee?" the suited man asked.

"Sure, follow me," the security guard replied.

As they got to the back steps at the rear of the building, the suited man observed: "The garbage smells horrible back here. Why haven't you cleaned it out?"

"Do I look like a garbage man to you, Lane?" the security guard replied in a very annoyed tone.

They quibbled a bit more amongst themselves, but Jay's attention was drawn to a movement immediately behind him.

Jay was paralyzed with fear. Something really bad was about to happen. However, he couldn't run, couldn't move, couldn't shout to warn the two men in front of him. Jay could only stand in terror and turn his head slightly to see what it was that landed behind him.

The reeking odor was not coming from garbage. It was coming from the *thing*! The thing that had landed behind them and oh so deathly close.

The image of a winged bat-like monster would be forever burned into the memory of Jay Christiano. It looked straight at him with hatred and disdain, but seemed to move through him as if he were not there.

The beast proceeded to attack the two men. It lifted the men into the air with a violent thrust and smashed both their heads together with such force that their heads splattered with a bloody rupture – like watermelons that had been hit with a sledgehammer.

"No!" Jay screamed, but his pleas did not stop the ultra-violence.

The monster was some kind of vampire and bit into the suited man with such hunger that it completely took off a big chunk of meat from the man's neck. Blood began squirting from the wound in uncontrolled sprits and the monster guzzled it with similar contempt, all the while glaring at Jay.

That was the first of many nightmares Jay Christiano would have.

***

"Whoa!" Jay woke with a startle again, sitting up straight in the strange motel bedroom he'd stopped over at on his multi-leg journey to Davis, West Virginia, and switched on the light. He rubbed his bleary eyes, sighed in relief to be awake again and away from the horrific visions of sleep, and squinted at the alarm clock. It was 03:03 a.m. Again. He yawned and threw off the sheets, then made his way to the bathroom.

While the soupy smell of his piss filled his nostrils, the freaky nightmare visions still filled his mind. *God! Were these getting worse?*

He tried to wipe out the memory, so recent and vivid, of another hellish scene he felt like he was living through, rather than dreaming about. He had no idea where these ideas were coming from. It wasn't like he'd watched horror movies recently, was on drugs, or reading anything like Dante's *Inferno*, but he was sure he was visiting some kind of hell world every night.

And every night, he tried to escape these nightmares. He played his iPod while he was in bed and listened to soothing classical music rather than the rock music he loved. He read comic books and humorous novels. Nothing heavy, scary or thought-provoking. He'd tried drinking to excess, drinking only warm milk, not eating cheese. He'd tried staying up so he was exhausted as well as having early nights so he was fresh. Still the same. It had been like this for weeks now, although he managed to be his bright, amiable self during the day. It was as if something happened at night to drive him to the edge of his sanity. Yet in the day, he was fine.

DECEMBER 23

The lights of Tulsa, Oklahoma appeared in the windshield in front of him. It was getting late. *Probably should stop here for the night,* he thought. *Hopefully, I can get some actual sleep.*

He had stopped at a couple of other motels to spend the night along the way and hoped that a change of scenery from home, and his tiredness from driving might give him some respite from his bad dreams. But no. Whenever he did fall asleep, he was beleaguered by the same horrific visions that tormented him in his dreams, and left him exhausted on awakening, as if he'd had no rest.

Every night, he dreamed various apocalyptic scenes of the end of the world – of a desolate, gray wasteland filled with sounds of screaming agony, of endless human suffering, and of terrible monsters lurking in the night. In his dreams, there were various plagues, torments and floods of Biblical proportions, and the air was thick with the stench of death and despair. The only way he could cope with the distressing sights was to remember that they were only dreams.

He had learned to practice lucid dreaming – to be aware during his dream-state that this was only his imagination, to have some kind of control over his own actions and feelings during the dream. Although he seemed powerless to stop them from occurring, at least he was protected from some of the pain and fear that he saw around him. But not all of it. As a compassionate man, he was still distressed by the level of anguish and agony he saw in this dream world that seemed so real.

Nights aside, this vacation was just what he needed. Jay enjoyed exploring towns he'd never been to. He visited local bars and diners, enjoying chatting with the regulars, who embraced the friendly guy's company. Even women felt safe with him, since he was neither a player nor looking for love. He never flirted or acted sleazy; he was just a regular guy, polite and pleasant.

Checking into the Hyatt Regency, he sensed an inviting atmosphere in the hotel's bar and decided to have a look around before grabbing his luggage from the car.

He saw a woman drinking water at the bar. She looked shabby, but was bright-eyed and friendly. They got to chatting, along with the bartender.

"Can I buy you a drink?" Jay asked, with such pleasantness that the woman knew he wasn't coming on to her.

"Oh, just a water, thank you!" she smiled, raising her glass.

"Do you mind my asking, but is there a reason why you're drinking water?" he asked in a low voice, pulling up a seat next to her.

"Oh... it's not that I'm an alcoholic," the woman blushed. "It's just..." she lowered her voice, embarrassed, "I like to pay my way. And I can't reciprocate, I'm afraid."

Jay smiled, touched by her honesty. He noticed the lady was dressed in a maid's outfit and realized she must be an off-duty housekeeper. "No problem. But let me buy you a drink anyway. I've had some good fortune, and I'd like to spread it a little. What would you really like to drink?"

She looked up at him, doubtful, but then saw the frankness in his eyes and trusted him. She said shyly, "Alright. A white wine, please."

Jay raised his finger to attract the bartender, who was away serving another customer. He approached, eyes bright with friendliness.

"Same again for me, and for the lady…"

"Water," the bartender assumed.

"Wine. Your finest white." He then turned to the woman and held out his hand. "Jay Christiano, just travelling through."

She took his hand and shook it in greeting, "Martha, just… stayin' here."

"I've been to your vineyard, Martha!" Jay joked.

They chatted for the rest of the evening.

When Jay stood to leave, Martha smiled in puzzlement. "Listen. It's refreshing to speak to a guy all evening that doesn't just want to get in my pants. Are you gay?"

"I'm just very happy," Jay reassured her, "And I have respect for women like yourself."

"Bless your heart, Jay Christiano." She raised her wine glass. "You're one in ten billion!"

Jay left the bar, warm and drowsy from the conversation and wine, and strolled through the hotel lobby, intending to return to his room for quiet contemplation before bed… and the nightmares that would inevitably follow.

Jay just enjoyed life as it was, and yeah, maybe in time he might settle down, but for now, he had too many things he wanted to achieve. Experiences he wanted to have...

Now THAT might be nice, he contemplated to himself as he stood in the lobby of his hotel perusing a sign advertising the hotel's spa services. "Open Late" it announced.

He took the elevator up to the Hyatt's relaxation therapy center and ordered himself a foot and leg massage, and a reflexology session. He loved driving, especially in the Mustang, but his feet and legs got cramped with so much time in a confined space, driving for hours, with just an odd bathroom stop along the way.

He lay on the couch in the therapy room, and closed his eyes, while the therapist, Maria, set to work stroking his feet with a fragrant wipe before pouring a handful of beautifully scented oils on her palms, massaging his feet and lower legs, rubbing his toes, pinching them one by one and pressing on certain acupressure points on the soles of his feet.

"Ahhh," he sighed, in some kind of ecstasy of relaxation. "Oh, that is so good!"

Maria smiled to herself, but remained silent. She worked instinctively, and from experience knew that some clients liked to chatter throughout their session, asking questions which she gladly answered, diagnosing various bodily ailments from the accumulation of crystals and characteristics she felt in the soles of his feet. Some clients liked to relax, and even sleep. She intuited that Jay, for all his friendliness, was one of the latter. So she simply pressed his flesh, smoothing out muscular aches and discrepancies with her strong fingers and thumbs.

The soothing, rhythmical touch, the relaxing ambient music, and the comfortable padded therapy couch ensured that Jay was soon so chilled that he slipped into something more comfortable – unconsciousness.

At first, he was lulled into a beautiful world of calm and peace. Then, as ever, the vision darkened to a shadowy landscape of destruction, filling him with unease. A metallic stench of blood was in the air, and he saw bodies piled in heaps like discarded garbage at a dump. White arms stuck pleadingly out of the pile, palms up in gestures of appeasement or pleading. He didn't know.

"This is not real. This is a dream. I'll wake up in a minute," he told himself, as he always did.

Although this mantra offered his sensitive mind and compassionate nature some reassurance, he still felt the horror of all he saw. Gray, oppressive figures in shadow terrorized the skeletal human forms he saw, who ran wailing and shrieking to escape. They never would, he knew instinctively. Worse, Jay felt powerless to help.

"This is not real. This is a dream. I'll wake up in a minute!" he chanted once again – this time with urgent intent – hoping that his words would give the tortured souls some hope, too. Everybody ignored him, as if he wasn't there, but their fear was palpable. He felt their pain, terror and despair.

Was this of his making? His imagination? Why was his mind making up such stuff?

"Why?!" he wailed, crying aloud so hard that he jerked awake, to find Maria, round-eyed, squeezing his feet at the end of the couch. More for her own safety than for his, he realized. She looked like she was clinging onto him for dear life! Her olive-skinned brow wrinkled in puzzlement and concern.

"Whoa!" he said, realizing where he was and what had happened. "Sorry! Nightmare!"

Maria slid her palms to the tops of his feet and held them there, warm and reassuring.

"D'you get them often?"

"Hmmm," he answered, embarrassed, "Most nights…"

"I'm sorry," said Maria, her brown eyes soft with concern. "And strangely, I don't pick up any stress from your feet."

"I don't think my feet have a lot of stress. Apart from carrying my body about!"

Maria laughed. "No. Every point on your feet connects to a part of your whole body. The big toe," she pointed to his first toe, "is like a microcosm of your head. But it feels fine to me. In fact, you're in great shape!"

"Thanks. You're in pretty great shape too!" he said innocently, as if merely returning the same compliment.

Maria smiled, refreshed by the fact that he wasn't even coming onto her. Many men – especially one-off clients and tourists, often asked her for "extras." She never did extra services, and often warned them, "There are no Happy Endings here! Unless you like getting banged up in a police cell!"

But she did, on occasion, share a certain extra service she gave, over which she had no control. She bit her lip, uncertain, but decided to go for it.

"Hey, I don't know how you feel about... well, the spirit world," she started, tentatively.

Jay frowned. *Did she know about his visions? Was she psychic?* He quickly rearranged his face to an expression of blank interest.

"Each to their own," he smiled. "I'm open-minded."

She gave a half smile and continued. "Well, I know it's crazy, but I'm a little... sensitive. I get feelings about people and things..." she paused, waiting for him to laugh or get offended. He simply sat patiently, waiting for the rest of her story.

She folded her soft hands on her lap before her. "Call it intuition if you like, or psychic mediumship, but I just feel..." she gulped, "You are meant for greatness!"

His eyebrows flickered quizzically.

"That's all I know. They're just telling me 'Meant for greatness.' You will do great things. I mean, great! Like, practically save the world!"

Now Jay really couldn't stop an ironic smile twisting his lip, but he said gently, not wanting to offend her, "You mean like Superman?"

She smiled, "I know – it sounds crazy, doesn't it? I just get the sense that you will face terrible, terrible things – and survive."

"Good to know – well, the survival bit, anyway!" Jay was careful not to sound too teasing, because this girl was earnest. She really believed what she was saying, even if he didn't.

"It's more than that. I can't explain." Maria was waving her skilled, expressive fingers in the air, as if she could pluck the appropriate words from there. "Just... bigger. Way bigger. Massive. But I don't know what. Just... like... sorry." She shrugged, apologetically.

"Okay," smiled Jay. "Thank you. That's nice."

"Perhaps you must save those who are suffering in your dreams."

"I think those folks may have already died," he replied.

"Then perhaps you are to avenge them," Maria countered. "Sorry I can't give you any more information," she said, her hands open, empty.

Jay paid her gratefully and left. Sweet girl, but maybe just over-imaginative.

Just like me! Jay laughed.

CHAPTER 5

Floyd Lake was a medium-sized manmade reservoir situated approximately five miles upstream from the town of Melas. It was originally the central water source for both Melas and neighboring Tarklin village in the early 1800s.

When settlers first moved to the area, they noticed the soil was incredibly fertile where Bridge Creek split off from the West Fork River. The West Fork was actually part of the Monongahela. Like many parts of West Virginia, the larger bodies of water – the rivers – became creeks, the creeks became streams, and the streams became brooks the farther one would ascend into the mountains.

In Floyd Lake's case, Graham Floyd thought the topography was just perfect to build a lake. Mr. Floyd was one of the early surveyors who worked on plotting the original U.S. Route 50 through the area and believed that if he dammed up this particular piece of Bridge Creek near where Raccoon Run jutted off to meet with Route 50, then settlers – farmers especially – could work the land downstream and there would always be water in reserve during dry years to keep the crops healthy.

Mr. Floyd sold his proposal to the Virginia legislators in Richmond and Floyd Lake was born. Had the Virginia legislators known in advance that years later, Fort Melas would spring up and that very lake would be used to give Union soldiers an upper hand in the region, perhaps they would have passed and built a lake elsewhere. Perhaps had Floyd Lake not been built at all, the Great Flood of West Virginia might not have happened. But then again...

***

The drive to Floyd Lake was five miles along a one-lane country road. The road wound back and forth through some woods, following the path of Bridge Creek right up to the dam. Folks would drive through the small town of Melas, turn onto Raccoon Run Road and drive for almost two miles, and then veer to the left fork that stayed with the valley along Bridge Creek.

Most townsfolk knew if they went right at the fork instead of left, the road would lead up a hill, past some houses, then eventually to a dead-end at the hill's peak. The spectacular Madison House was perched at the top of the hill overlooking the town of Melas to the front and if one were to go around to the back side of the Madison House, they could see Floyd Lake nestled between some hills not too far below the perch that the house was sitting on.

To someone who was not from Melas, the person might be inclined to believe that Floyd Lake was part of the Madison property – a private lake or fishing retreat for the wealthy person who happened to reside in the abode. However, this was not the case and if one did in fact go left, they would discover, as many often did, the winding Bridge Creek would lead them up, up, and up to the base of the dam and a small public parking area.

Seen from down below, the dam at Floyd Lake looked like a massive mound of overgrown rubble, the work of a glacier perhaps. It rose up almost 90 feet above the valley floor and was an impressive 800 feet long. The dam's face was very steep and covered with loose rocks. There were deep crevices between the rocks where patches of weeds, poison ivy, and juniper had long since taken root, sprouting aggressively, and giving the impression that this "hill of rocks" actually belonged to the natural landscape.

As decades rolled on, there was hardly any signs that this hill – this dam – was the work of man, and no inkling at all of what lay on the other side, except over at the far right where a spillway had been cut through the solid rock of the hillside and water came crashing down over large, dark stones below.

In years gone by, many lovers would visit this locale on date nights to romance under this picturesque waterfall. Many young women lost their virginity within earshot of the crashing water. Similarly, this was a prime party spot and on any given day, one could expect to see the area littered with beer bottles, cans, used condoms and various other discarded packages.

Beyond the parking spot at the base of the falls, a metal bridge crossed the noisy water and directed the road straight up to a patch of pine trees at the top of the dam, just beyond the far right of the lake and the spillway. If a person drove up this steep incline and looked left, the dam dropped off a great deal more abruptly than it had looked from below. This was the highest point in the region with the exception of the nearby hill that showcased the Madison House.

Of course, things do change with time and the grandeur of the Madison estate was no more. Where a stately manor once stood was only a chimney now. In the subsequent inferno that destroyed the structure, a multi-acre forest fire had wiped out most of the surrounding vegetation as well as several houses on the same side of Bridge Creek. It was one of the worst fires in West Virginia history and took six fire departments to eventually put out the blaze.

Nowadays, where a once pristine evergreen patch of woods adorned a lakeside, the pine trees were burnt husks and the landscape was charred and desolate. Very few people ever came up here now and this particular holiday season, the pouring rain and snow mix added exponentially to the overall feeling of dystopia. Large thunderheads rumbled across the valley in ever-increasing intervals.

A lone figure parked his late-model black Cadillac near the edge of the dam and got out. There was not another soul around Floyd Lake that Christmas Eve. The man walked around to the back of his car and opened up the trunk. He pulled out a large duffel bag. In it were scuba gear and a metal, egg-shaped canister that was similar in shape and size to a football.

The man looked out on the lake. Waves crashed restlessly on the shore and over the spillway. The water was very high this evening. It was reported that during the wet spring months, Floyd Lake covered over 300 acres and was over 80 feet deep in places.

"It may not be spring," Talman Cane said with a huff as he lifted the small, but rather heavy "egg" from the trunk, "but that don't mean shit when it comes to flash floods, does it Dad?" Talman let out a sinister laugh that would cause any onlooker to question his sanity, especially since there was no one else around. Talman didn't care. He figured "Dad" would hear him. He usually did. And this year, Talman had just the appropriate Christmas gift for his dear father. He hoped "Dad" would be pleased. He suspected he would be.

Talman's father wasn't the only person he would speak with this evening.

"That's one mighty big body of water up there on the mountain! Wouldn't you agree, McClumpy?" Talman asked himself.

"Yes, a mighty big body indeed!" Talman replied in a different voice.

Talman did not *suffer* from multiple personality disorder. Rather, he quite enjoyed it and was well aware of all the personalities in his head. He never could be completely comfortable being one person all of the time. His true nature was evil and unpredictable. But sometimes – and usually by accident – he would possess the bodies of individuals who were the exact opposite, as was the case of Mr. Josef McClumpy. Talman found it very fascinating to hold conversations between himself and the person whose body he possessed.

Of course, the soul of Josef McClumpy was long since dead and in hell, but that didn't stop Talman Cane from role playing – especially since Talman was all alone up on the lake and needed someone to talk to.

This was one of the few times Talman could be himself. In public, the roles were reversed. He had to be Josef McClumpy – the upright, kind funeral home director who was always in the public eye and always there to lend a sympathetic ear to grieving families. Never once did he let on that the person they were confiding in was not Josef McClumpy, but rather a sociopathic, demonic creature who had killed the real Josef McClumpy two years prior and assumed the man's entire life.

Talman had no other choice. Ever since the tapes of Jimbo Wilders went public and implicated him in several murders, Talman had to change identities. For an immortal, that didn't mean simply moving out of town or using a different ID. Talman literally *changed*.

Unfortunately for the person being "assumed" it meant death, but Talman didn't mind. As long as Talman was okay, that's all that mattered. And in Talman's warped mind, he felt that having a conversation with the "host" every now and then would keep that person's essence alive.

"I bet that water is cold!" Talman exclaimed.

"You ain't a-kiddin'!" McClumpy replied. "I saw on the Caddy's thermostat coming over here that it had dropped below thirty degrees!"

"Well you better not fuck around down there or you'll end up freezing your nuts off!" Talman warned.

"Can't have shrinkage, TC." McClumpy replied.

"No. We certainly cannot. But, think of the positive – after today your funeral business will be set for the entire year!"

"I love your clever business mind."

"Now, hurry the fuck up and get into that swim suit!"

***

The difference in elevation from the dam at the top of Floyd Lake to the village of Tarklin some seven miles downstream was 500 feet. In the middle was Melas at nearly 300 feet. Unlike Melas, which had only Bridge Creek running through it, Tarklin was situated at the confluence of Bridge Creek and Elk Creek, where the two flowed together and connected with the West Fork. It was almost ten miles from the dam to the West Fork and the water in Floyd Lake was approximately 15 million gallons. Indeed, it was one big body of water up there on the mountain.

The hard, cold rain that had started coming down on December 20 had changed to a wintry mix of sleet and snow by 4:00 p.m. that afternoon. After four days of one hundred percent humidity, the banks were well above flood stage and Floyd Lake was nearing its brim on Christmas Eve.

Water from Floyd Lake was regulated by both the spillway and a catch basin that was connected to a discharge pipe. The catch basin was roughly fifty feet out in the lake and the top of it could usually be seen peeking above the surface of the water. The discharge pipe plunged straight down into the base of the dam and helped relieve pressure from the spillway and prevent the dam from overflowing. This evening the catch basin was nowhere to be seen.

Talman knew the approximate location of the catch basin, as he had been up here on numerous occasions. Thus, he did not really need to see it to know it was there. He also knew that the cast iron grate that sat on top of the basin could be lifted off if one was strong enough. McClumpy as a mortal may or may not be able to yank off the grate, but with Talman Cane running things, he was confident that he could pull it off.

Once in the wetsuit, Talman quickly splashed into the choppy water and swam out to the basin. The water was abnormally rough and the turbulence made Talman wonder for a moment if he would be able to complete what he came here for.

Talman had anticipated being in the lake and out in about two minutes. Unfortunately he did not find the grate until he had been swimming around for ten minutes. By that time, he was very cold and no longer joking with his alternative personality.

With a giant heave, he yanked the grate away from the catch basin and let it sink into the murky depths below. Next, he repositioned a swimmers pack he was wearing so that he could extract its contents. The "egg" was inside.

Once he dropped the egg, Talman knew that he would have approximately thirty seconds to swim back to the shore and at least get out of the water before it went off. His plan was that whatever sound it made would be ignored – either by being muffled by the water or attributed to the thunder that had been rolling through the valley all afternoon. He wasn't sure if anyone would take notice, but by now he didn't care.

Talman steadily balanced the egg on the edge of the catch basin. He knew that one of two outcomes were about to play out. Once he dropped the egg, it would either explode and blow out the discharge hole, which in turn would cause a large amount of water to gush out of the lake, or the discharge hole would implode – sealing off the hole and causing Floyd Lake to overflow. The former would drain out the lake over a couple days and the latter would possibly cause the entire dam to collapse – especially if water flowed over the top of the dam instead of just the spillway.

"Can't dwell on the possibilities while freezing my ass off!" Talman exclaimed as he activated the egg and dropped it down the hole into the aquatic depths below.

CHAPTER 6

The few remaining workers left alive at the Weston State Lunatic Asylum worked frantically to get control of an already out-of-control situation. The Harrison County Sheriff and his deputy lay on the floor in a pool of blood. Doors along the main wing of the complex were flung open and no one standing even dared to go down and investigate.

They knew that if they looked in any one of these patient rooms, they would see dead bodies everywhere. Vampire ghouls had ransacked the place, eating the patients indiscriminately in their mindless search for blood and flesh.

On top of that, a young boy who had come to visit his mother earlier this evening – on Christmas Eve – lay dead. Cathy Edwards screamed madly and inconsolably in the Gothic mental hospital where the group stood.

"I can't take this anymore, Johnny!" Amanda said. "Please get me out of here."

She dropped a butcher knife she had been holding and grabbed both of his arms with such force that Jonathan Harker thought she might actually draw blood. He shuddered. The last thing he needed was to be bleeding if one more of those ghouls were to appear from out of nowhere. He definitely did not need to be on their menu.

"Sweetheart, how can we go anywhere?" he asked. The weather had gotten worse over the past several hours that they had been "stuck" at Weston.

Pete, one of the male nurses, looked up from his station. "He's got a point. The local news is reporting the West Fork River rising over one foot per hour. They don't know when it's going to stop. You guys better stay here and wait for the authorities. Besides, *somebody* is going to have to explain this mess!"

William took a worried glance over at the body of Ralphie Edwards. His mother was down on the floor next to him. "Come back, come back! Oh God, please come back! You can't die, not now!"

William looked back to Jonathan and whispered, "Do you think he's really dead?"

"I sure as hell hope so!" Jonathan replied.

"I mean, the demon's gone, so he should be dead, right?"

"You're the priest."

William clutched the crucifix that was still dangling from his hand. "The only way to be sure – really sure – is to finish him off."

Amanda interjected, "Willie, you can't be serious. He's dead and there's nothing more we can do."

"Actually, there is," William replied. "We can drive a stake through his heart and cut off his head!" He shot Ralphie another look, this time more determined than before.

Jonathan watched in utter shock as William dropped to the floor to retrieve Amanda's discarded

70

butcher knife. "Hold on buddy." Jonathan protested. "We can't do it; not now. And not with all these people around." This time it was his turn to whisper. "There are too many witnesses."

"Well, just for the record," William replied, "if he was a vampire, and that's sure what he looked like to me, I cannot guarantee he won't come back to life and eat these people."

Amanda looked panicked. "And *that's* all the more reason we need to get out of here. NOW!" She pulled Jonathan closer to her by his shirt. "Johnny, please. I wish we had never left Canada. I wish we were back in the hotel, or anywhere but here."

Brief visions of his first romantic encounter with Amanda Davenport flashed through Jonathan Harker's head. She had a point. It wasn't too terribly long ago he had lost his first real love, Lucy Westerna, to a vampire in Melas, only a few miles from where they now stood. He was beginning to develop similar feelings towards Amanda and he would be damned if he was going to stay there to be slaughtered, if, in fact, more ghouls were coming from the basement.

He was also aware of Amanda's unwilling incarceration in the Weston State Lunatic Asylum when she was seventeen. *That had to be traumatic for her,* Jonathan thought to himself. *Plus, the way she was about to go after Dr. Henry Cane – Holy crap!*

"Okay. Let's go!" Jonathan announced.

Nurse Pete was out of earshot and attending to the screaming Edwards woman fifty feet down the hall.

"Let's quickly get to the door and not announce we are leaving!"

The trio swiftly moved through the front lobby and out the door into the freezing town outside.

***

Dr. Cane was so mad, he could not see straight. His jet black Hummer sped wildly through the night towards Tarklin. His brother better have some answers! He was well aware that Ralphie and Legion would eventually show up at the asylum where he worked. That was a given, being that Ralphie's mom was a patient. *But what the hell happened back there?* he wondered.

The Hummer drove through roughly six inches of water that had made its way over the bridge that tied one side of Weston to the other where the asylum was situated. Cane didn't care – that's why he drove a Hummer.

The snow–rain mix had made the roads a sheet of ice and the Hummer skidded off the road, bounced into a berm, and back on again. Pulling onto the interstate, Cane even did a donut before regaining control of the vehicle and pointing it in the right direction – North – toward Tarklin. Luckily for Cane, there was no traffic on the roadways this night.

He would have his answers and less than an hour later, he pulled into his brother's driveway.

A furious pounding literally shook the ornate oak door practically off the hinges of the McClumpy mansion. Henry Cane angrily sneered at the security camera and stuck out his middle finger to anyone who happened to be watching.

"Aah brother," Talman said jovially, trying to defuse the situation as he opened the door. "It's awfully nice of you to come to clean the snow off my sidewalks! Especially at 2:00 a.m."

Henry Cane pushed past his brother, not caring that he was trudging thick clumps of snow into his brother's foyer and then onto his plush living room carpets as he flung himself onto the nearest couch.

"Tell me Talman, or Josef, or whatever-the-fuck-your-name-is-now, why did Legion decide to attack *my* place of employment?"

"You'll have to ask him that question yourself the next time you chat. It is not my fault that Weston is downstream from Melas. Perhaps it was just coincidence."

"Coincidence my ass!" Henry remarked. "These are modern times, Talman. You cannot just waltz into a fucking hospital and slaughter a bunch of people while another group watch!"

"I see YOU made it out okay," his brother replied.

"Yes, but that place is a mess. People will be looking for answers. Soon, they'll be looking for *me*. Wondering where I ran off to."

"'Ran off' you say?" Talman replied.

"I didn't have a choice. Legion made a real mess of things and I didn't have time to stick around."

"Fret not, dear brother. If you lose your job at Weston, at least you have the part-time gig at the Water Board."

"Fuck off. I like my job at the asylum."

"And I'm sure you'll get things straightened out. You always do."

"That's not all." Henry replied. "The fae has returned."

"Fae?" Talman smirked. "You mean a fairy, like Tinkerbell? Brother, are you on drugs?"

"Don't smart-ass me, Talman. I am not in the mood."

"I'm just trying to figure out if I heard you correctly. You said a 'fae,' right?"

"Do you have any booze around here?" Henry asked, standing back up, taking off his wet jacket and flinging it onto an ornate end table nearby.

"Anything for you, brother," Talman replied with a sigh as he moved quickly to yank the overcoat from the table before it left water stains. "You will find a wide assortment of adult beverages in the cabinet near the kitchen..."

"I'll help myself," Henry interrupted.

Moments later, he came back with two glasses and a bottle of brandy. "It's been a long night, Talman. Here." He tossed one of the glasses at his brother, and fortunately Talman was quick enough to grab it in mid air before the crystal smashed to the floor.

"Nice catch," Henry remarked.

"I suppose it was, for being two in the morning and all," Talman replied.

Henry poured a drink for the two of them and sat back down on the couch. He had regained some of his composure, but Talman could see that his brother was still very angry and equated him with a powder keg capable of blowing up at any time. As he sipped his liquor, he felt it best not to joke anymore with him this morning.

"Anyway, the business with the fae," Henry started. "A few years back, there was this teenage girl; seventeen or eighteen years old; very attractive. She wasn't the typical mental patient that I am accustomed to seeing. Her dad was tired of seeing her around, so he had her locked up."

"In your tender care, I presume?" Talman interjected.

"Indeed." Henry replied. That brought his first smile of the visit. "She was spunky and we started having to keep her in restraints around the clock."

"Poor girl, but I'm sure you didn't mind."

"Not really. Not at first. But a few days into her evaluation something odd happened."

Talman, who was in mid sip, raised an eyebrow from behind the glass.

"I felt a punch from her *spirit* while she lay on the table. This has never happened before, but as clear as the day, I felt as if some supernatural manifestation jumped from her body and hit me. Hell, it about knocked me down!"

Henry finished off his glass and poured himself another. "Neither of us were around in the times of the Ancient Persian Empire – the time when the necromancers were mighty and the vampires were created." He continued, "Your buddy Rothenstein knew some of those very necromancers. The obelisk that he brought over here was created by such folk. Do you know what it represents?"

"A gateway to hell," Talman replied matter-of-factly.

"Yes!" exclaimed Henry. "But that's not all. There was a great war between the vampires and 'The Winged Ones' as Rothenstein called them. *He* – Rothenstein – was in that very war and told me this story himself!

"The vampires won – barely – and only with the help of the necromancers. The necromancers gained the upper hand by building bridges – gates – to the netherworld and summoning the darkest of evil to come to the aid of the vampires."

"That's a little deep for me, Brother," Talman said. "I was A LOT better friends with Victor Rothenstein and it sure is funny he never mentioned this battle of the ages to me."

"Perhaps he didn't think you cared," Henry replied. "Walther Pinkman was a necromancer and he called The Winged Ones 'fae.' We talked for hours on the matter before he passed away.

"He explained how the vampires experienced an acute pain unlike any they had ever known when a fae would strike – a terrible freezing and paralysis. The fae would then use this moment to sever the vampire's head and finish off their victim once and for all.

"Walter confided in me that he could not imagine all of the faes in existence were eradicated during the great war. Most of the necromancers did die and with them, the secrets of the obelisk. Victor Rothenstein was one of the few remaining creatures of that time to take possession of the obelisk and hide it away. He never really knew how to open the gateway, but always relished the idea of keeping the artifact close by no matter where he was."

"I know the obelisk is a gateway to hell, as Ralphie and Legion have clearly shown," Talman affirmed. "But with us having direct commune with our father, Lucifer, I never paid it more attention than that. Father made no mentioned of The Winged Ones, fae, or whatever they are, and I never felt their presence."

"Of course not!" Henry replied. "And that is because they were defeated and driven from this earth. Fragments of their spirits remain in folklore, especially Anglo Saxon, but I could see you never cared to pursue it."

"So, if you don't mind me being so blunt as to ask: Why the fuck are we talking about this shit now and how come you believe an extinct race is now giving you grief?"

Henry finished off his second glass and poured himself a third. "I have two words for you: Toad Road."

"You never did tell me that story, Brother." Talman inquired.

"You were off in India at the time, but since the matter is before us now, I will tell you.

"In the 1800s, I had worked at Toad Road Asylum in York, Pennsylvania before moving on to Germany, and later, to here. Toad Road Asylum was a colossal mental asylum standing in Hellam woods, off of Toad Road. It had been the ideal place for my work, with hundreds of patients pretty much abandoned by their families, few laws and rules restricting my abilities, and a taboo about 'lunatics' which meant that nobody much cared or interfered. And better still, it was close to The Seven Gates of Hell. Not the same as our singular obelisk gateway here in Melas – these were a newer magick.

"These seven gates provided a portal to the underworld, which was extremely convenient for my intercessions with our Father, and we were only mildly irritated by occasional 'dare-devils' attempting to break through. The great thing about legends, and gullible people before the nineteenth century, was that most people lived in fear of the legend! The gates stood in the woods that run off Trout Run Road, which is the new name they gave to Toad Road after the fire.

"There was a local legend that if a human walked through the Seven Gates, they would go straight to hell, but no human being has ever made it past the fifth. The First Gate is rusted and warped iron with a loose, rotten wood frame and difficult to see, half concealed by undergrowth at a bend in the road. Gates Two through Seven could only be seen after nightfall, and were invisible during the day.

"On the left, there is a large clearing in a circle shape that covens of 'Wiccans' use for meetings and ceremonies. I prefer to call them witches. This ridiculous twenty-first-century language! Witches have been witches since before we were born in 1691. And we should know – our mother was one, after all!

"Back to Toad Road Asylum. Halcyon days of freedom, where I was at liberty to conduct the most precocious and dangerous of experiments, unassailed. Until I encountered the fae. I recognized her immediately, although her ghostly wings and pale blue aura can be seen by very few. Fortunately, she did not see me or recognize me for who I was. Reckless in my youth, being less than two hundred years old, which is still infancy for us cambions, I instinctively and immediately killed her before she could kill me.

"When certain faes die, they emit an energy force that is so powerful that it explodes into fire and incinerates all that is nearby. I learned that the hard way, and before my very eyes, a vast and extensive shaft of fire erupted like a volcano and tore through the center of the asylum. I truly know the meaning of 'spread like wildfire,' because I was thrown several hundred yards, blasted straight through the thick walls, and landed in the woods outside, lucky to escape with my eyebrows.

"Being in a remote locality, and no telephones being invented, no firefighters were able to assist when the asylum caught fire. Many patients had burned to death there, especially those locked in their rooms on the upper floors. Hundreds of others escaped into the woods surrounding the building. Local people were frightened of 'lunatics' and sent out lynch mobs of extraordinary violence, beating most of the patients they found, and killing others. The screaming souls of the dead still haunt the place.

"So that's what can happen when you commit such a simple act as to kill an unsuspecting fae."

"Damn!" Talman exclaimed. "And you just up and let her go – just like that."

"I had decided to play it safe. After all, I was never aware of this woman before she came here, despite her living close by, and she would be sure to avoid this place in the future after her time here with me. She would never harm me, since she was oblivious to her potential. As the saying goes, it might be best to 'let sleeping dogs lie.' However, it also meant that I could no longer experiment on her. What if I accidentally killed her during an experiment? Or what if my interventions unleashed a sudden knowing of her powers? I could not take that risk.

"I immediately declared her completely cured and had her discharged from the hospital, hoping to never see her again."

"But..." Talman said, waving his hand to force his brother to complete the thought.

"That was before she showed up tonight. She arrived with the County Sheriff, some man, and a teenage boy. I do not really know why they were there, but Ralphie Edwards also showed up at the same time!"

"Was he with them?" Talman asked.

"No. Ralphie came to me. I don't know how he got there. The weather is shit outside. Legion must have accelerated things. But Ralphie – the boy – still swayed the great demon to let him see his mom."

"Oh fuck," Talman replied. "I know where you are going with this. It's on the news."

Henry looked stunned, "Surely not! The hospital incident?"

"No. The mine."

Henry looked confused.

Talman picked up a remote control and turned on the television in the living room where they sat. A live feed from the WBOY news desk was being broadcast showing an ongoing incident at the Dark Hollows Mine.

A tired-looking Dirk McCallahan was on the screen reading some papers on the desk: "*... and right now, only one body has been retrieved from the mine. This just in: the access bridge on Dark Hollow Road leading to the mine has just washed out. I repeat, the bridge leading to the mine is no longer there. Hope is quickly fading for the trapped miners in these flooded conditions...*"

"Let me guess," Talman asked, "you haven't been following the news?"

"I was *distracted* tonight. Why?"

"The undead that Ralphie and Legion were conjuring up were not from the obelisk. They were from this mine. Jimbo fucked us on this!"

"What in the world are you talking about?" asked Henry.

"Jimbo Whilders. You know – our buddy who helped us get rid of Rothenstein's victims?"

"Yes. I am *very* familiar with him. He's the reason you had to change identities after he clearly identified you as his chief accomplice in all those serial killings."

"Yeah, *that* Jimbo." Talman sneered. "Anyway, he didn't do the job of completely decapitating the girls after Rothenstein drained them. He merely dumped their bodies down a mineshaft over at Runners Ridge.

"These undead vampire ghouls somehow escaped into the Dark Hollow Mine operation and they swam downstream to meet their leader, Legion."

"Who just so happened to be in the body of Ralphie as he was visiting dear old mom in my hospital," Henry deduced.

"Bingo."

"Well, just so you know, Legion was exorcised from Ralphie Edwards tonight and most of the ghouls were killed."

"Son of a bitch!" Talman exclaimed. "Exorcised? They had a fucking priest with them?"

Henry nodded.

"Motherfucker!" Talman cursed. "Tell me, did they administer the true death to Ralphie?"

"I don't know. I jetted when things starting going south. The fae-woman had murderous intent in her eyes, was holding a butcher knife, and I could not risk a duel in front of my employees and patients."

"Whatever!" Talman replied, waiving both hands in the air in exasperation. The remaining brandy in his glass flew into the air and onto his carpet. Now he was angry. "Henry, we've got to get our asses back to Weston pronto and reverse the exorcism before the sun comes up AND before the hospital washes away!"

"Washes away?"

"I'll tell you en route."

CHAPTER 7

The West Fork River is 103 miles long and runs through the towns of Monongah, Shinnston, Lumberport, Clarksburg, and Weston. The river drains about 800 square miles, pervading the heart of West Virginia, travelling across Marion, Harrison, Lewis, and Upshur counties, fed by tributaries such as Bingamon Creek; Tenmile, Booths, Elk, Simpson, Lost and Kincheloe creeks, like veins feeding arteries. Watersheds offered drainage to the creeks, which pass through narrow, deep hollows. From those hollows, highland streams rush down until they collect in lowland rivers and brooks.

The riverbeds were initially shallow and dammed by mill owners to power their watermills, making it un-navigable by anything larger than a canoe or flatboat. In 1793, Virginia chartered an improvement company for the river, which required milldam owners to install chutes so that boats could pass downstream. By 1800, the West Fork River was declared a navigable public highway. In 1817 the Monongahela Navigation Company planned to build a slack-water navigation system on the West Fork, with dams, chutes, and locks. By 1824, the works were damaged by a severe flood, when the project was abandoned.

When the Weston Asylum was constructed in 1850, Irish and German laborers and stonemasons came over to work on the project. Stone was quarried from the West Fork riverbed in order to provide the building materials for the asylum, thereby widening and deepening the river in areas, and worsening its propensity to develop into flood plains.

Flooding is a recurring problem. In 1950, the West Fork at Weston reached more than twenty-five feet, over eight feet above the flood stage. And the great storm in November 1985 resulted in six to seven inches of rain around Weston, Clarksburg, and Fairmont within a day. The West Fork at Weston crested at twenty-four feet, and severe flooding occurred overnight. In West Virginia, forty-seven people were killed in the flood of 1985.

***

Jonathan, Amanda, and William had hurried across the snowy landscape, unseen by anyone in the asylum. The deep snow was rapidly melting under their feet and turned from the crisp crunch of a few hours earlier to the deep wet slush of their escape route.

The quickest and most direct route to the perimeter fence was skirting the huge gothic building at the front, passing the archway, which opened into the courtyard, crossing over the grassed area now covered in deep but softening snow, and to the banks of the West Fork River. And from there, onto the access bridge that would lead to freedom.

As a result of the quarrying of the riverbed, the West Fork River near the asylum was consequently already abnormally wide, and to make matters worse was now in a flood stage. The suddenly thawing snow, and the drizzling rain that had now begun, added to the volume of water. The quick thaw and a heavy rain had begun in the south, and torrents of water from upstream had joined the usually slow-flowing West Fork River, adding to its speed and volume, and bringing in its deepening waters all manner of flotsam.

Barely realizing what they were doing, Jonathan and the others took the easiest route they could find through the snowfields. They followed the trench in the snow that the ghouls had made on their grotesque march from the river towards the asylum. In this direction, it fortuitously led them to the gap in the wire fence that gave them access to the riverside.

"Jesus!" cried Jonathan, looking beyond the fence, through to the rushing, icy waters a few feet away from them. The river was swollen beyond its banks.

"Blasphemy, Johnny!" said William, now that his priesthood was out in the open.

"It's okay," Amanda interjected. "There's a bridge a little way along the bank, and it leads to the road!"

"If we don't get swept off our feet first!" Jonathan said, wryly, staring at the rushing waters.

They tramped along the snowy bank, clinging close to the fence where the river was at its widest, for fear of slipping within the icy flow. Then the river meandered off away from the fence, providing them with an expanse that they could walk over with ease.

"There it is!" Amanda pointed triumphantly in the distance to the uprights of the access bridge, and the three renewed their hope, motivated to tramp faster through the slush, despite the biting pain of the cold and the driving rain.

Jonathan looked admiringly at Amanda. She was resilient! Many a woman he had been with would have been complaining that the rain was spoiling their hair, or the cold was killing them. She just worked through it, with her long hair plastered to her head and her make-up long ago washed off, but still pretty, for sure. He watched her as he walked behind her, noting her clothes clinging so wetly to her that they accentuated her shapely form.

They hurried across the wet land, heading directly for the bridge, careless that their speed was now kicking up great splashes in the muddy plain. Within fifty yards of the bridge, they were over their ankles in water, and stopped dead in horror.

Water was over the bridge. Worse still, fallen trees had been swept downstream by the flow. Along with large chunks of ice and swiftly moving currents, they had broken through the bridge supports, taking part of the platform with them. Traveling across the access bridge was impossible.

"Holy crap!" Amanda exclaimed.

"Auntie!" William scolded, but his piety was outweighed by his despair.

Jonathan added to the chorus: "Just when escape was in sight! Wouldya believe it!"

Panic was rising within them, reaching thin needling fingers into each of their hearts. None of them wanted to show the others how desperate they felt.

"Can we use the remains of the bridge?" asked William, trying to find a solution. "Can we get as far as we can, wading on the bridge surface? Maybe swim between the gap?"

"No, Willie." Jonathan patted the youth on the shoulder. "The bridge is already under water, likely to loosen any time now. Besides – have you seen all that crap busting through it? It would be too dangerous."

William took another look at the floating debris that rushed by, finding its way through the broken bridge.

"Shit! Fucking holy shit and Christ!" swore Willie, crossing himself. "Help us!"

Amanda's gaze was scouring the area, looking for alternatives and solutions to their dilemma. The bridge? No way. Swimming? Madness. Walking on, further down the river? Too far, too long, and making them too vulnerable if any of the evil powers that had decimated the Asylum chose to pursue them.

Across the land, she could see only snow and graying, watery ice, revealing its muddy under-depths. The river, too, swept by with a gray and icy sheen, speckled with tree branches, lengths of wood, polythene, pieces of sheet metal and boards, a plastic baby bath, bobbing on the surface at speed. All manner of crazy stuff, natural, manmade and undefinable, was speeding in the downflow, getting trapped or slowed down by the remains of the bridge, or crashing through the gap.

At their side of the bank, Amanda's eye caught a large area of boarded wood, about eight feet by eight feet that had been swept ashore. It looked substantial, like a piece of a dock that had been smashed off, floated downstream, and now had washed to their side of the bank. It backed up to a whole array of other objects: rigid plastic water containers, a kayak smashed beyond use.

Could they...? Would they be able to take advantage of what the river had brought them? Amanda thought fast.

"Look!" she pointed to the tangle of flotsam, and the wedge of wooden platform. "Can we use that?"

As if he'd read her mind, Jonathan was already wading out to the barrage of junk. William splashed down in his wake, followed by Amanda, and all of them heaved the small platform out onto the muddy bank. It was a square of densely tight boards, screwed to a couple of substantial joists, and once they had untangled it from the other crap, and pulled it into the shallows, it floated safely. Jonathan tested his weight on it and it held him and he grinned in relief. William went back to the dammed up junk for a tangle of blue nylon rope and two plastic water containers he'd spotted.

"To help us float!" he explained.

"Yeah, Mandy – I reckon we can use this to make a raft to ford the river," grinned Jonathan, his eyes lit up with enthusiasm for the first time that day. "It's already floated this far, pretty intact!"

"Can we get across the river with it? How will we steer?" asked Amanda, thinking ahead, looking in the direction of the road on the other side of the river. It was covered in snow, so the small access road that led to the main highway was invisible. But she knew it was there. Taunting. So close, yet impossibly unreachable.

"Hell, do we care if we get to the main road? I don't care if we're swept way downriver, long as we're miles away from here!" Jonathan exclaimed.

True, Amanda conceded. Any place was better than here.

Amanda joined in with William, lashing the water containers to the sides of the platform. If it stopped the makeshift raft from flipping over in the current, it was worth a try. Her frozen fingers had long ago lost all feeling, like the dead weights of her feet, and she tied knots by sight rather than touch, her hands like raw meat attachments on the end of her arms. She fought to contain the trembling.

It's not fear! It's the cold! She told herself, over and over. Trying to convince herself.

Jonathan came back with a couple of lengths of wood.

"What's that for?" asked William, shaking with the cold himself, kneeling in the icy water to tie a large empty aluminum container that he'd found bobbing against the debris and recovered to provide more buoyancy to the raft. He couldn't feel any of his body below his hips. *Ah, well. I'm not sure I wanted kids anyway,* he thought. *Although they do freeze sperm, so maybe I'll be okay – if I live that long!*

"Thought we might need something to steer with." Jonathan perused the two-by-four and the long flexible pole he had retrieved from the nest of branches and broken buildings that was threatening the bridge. "If I can't use oars, I'll shunt us along. Pretend we're in Venice on one of those gondola things. You two can just lie back and relax. I'll stand up with a length of wood, singing opera and acting like a gondolier."

Jonathan's attempts to make a joke made no impression whatsoever on his two friends, who stood up one by one and stepped back to study their handiwork.

"Will it do, Johnny?" asked William, his brow furrowed with worry.

"Sure! Looks great to me."

"Babe, I'm not sure I'm getting your happy-happy vibes," Amanda muttered. "Personally, I'd rather you were shit-scared like the rest of us. I could trust that!"

Jonathan's false grin dropped. "Okay. But seriously – it looks fine. Let's test it out."

"We need to get it to the other side beyond the bridge, right?" asked William, bending with the others to carry the raft deeper into the water.

"No, Willie, we need to set it off this side, ram the bridge and get funneled through the broken bridge with all the lumber and shit!" Jonathan answered, sarcastically.

"Maybe I prefer you pretending to be happy," William murmured, and they half floated, half lifted the raft around the flooded bridge access, facing downstream.

They were now knee deep in freezing cold water, walking on land that should have been grass but was now underwater, and level with the entrance onto the broken bridge. They were just beginning to feel the gentle tug of the current from the water that flowed around the blockage of the bridge and the dam of debris.

"Once we get further out, it'll be wild. Let's get on here now, and I'll scoot it further midstream once we're all aboard," said Jonathan, holding the raft steady with his weight, while William clambered on, the raft dipping and bobbing with his weight, and hauled his aunt on board. Water sloshed over the surface of the raft, but just as quickly ran through the slim gaps between the boards or followed the grooves to waterfall off the ends.

Jonathan passed William the lengths of wood he aimed to use to push them into safety, and then set about mounting the platform himself. Although her attention was mostly focused on Jonathan swinging his leg over the raft, from the corner of her eye Amanda saw a gray log floating towards them.

"Oh!" she cried, realizing that being rammed by a tree trunk could finish them off before they started.

Jonathan swung his front leg off the raft and into the wet depths of the muddy riverbank again so he could push the raft back inland out of the log's way, while William, with all his might, pushed off the raft in the same direction.

Weirdly, the log veered off to the side too, and came towards them diagonally, rather than being swept in a straight-line way beyond them with the midstream flow. Now that it was closer, Amanda could see that it wasn't a log, but a bundle of rags.

"It's okay. Jump back aboard," she begged Jonathan. "It's not solid. No danger!"

Trusting her, Jonathan swung his upper body over the raft, while William grabbed his arms, and Jonathan hitched his leg up onto the platform again. The gray rags disappeared beneath the raft.

"What?" Jonathan cried in bewilderment.

Jonathan's remaining foot was stuck on something in the water. His eyes widened in surprise, as William and Amanda took an arm each to drag him on, and he found he couldn't lift himself entirely up. Most of his body lay on the raft, but his lower leg was caught on something – weeds or debris? He kicked out his trailing leg, trying to release it from whatever he was stuck on.

Amanda let out an ear-piercing screech, and William swiftly swung the length of two-by-four over Jonathan's head.

"What the...? You crazy?" said Jonathan, surging forward with the propulsion of his straining leg suddenly being released. He fell chin-first on the far side of the raft, before scrambling onto his knees and looking behind him.

Feet away from them, the head and shoulders of a person seated in the shallows were visible. Long gray hair was slicked black and wet across his or her face, but the head swung round, flinging back the ropes of greasy hair, and Jonathan almost gagged.

The face was greenish gray: a ghastly inhuman pallor; but worse was the swinging, wizened and red eyeball dangling on its cheek, hanging from a gristly string from the dark red, gaping eye socket. At least Jonathan thought that was worst, until he saw the thing open its huge, wet, red razor-teethed mouth and give out an unearthly screech.

Amanda countered that with a shriek of her own, before shouting, "Fuck! *Fuck*! Get the hell out!"

William was the first to recover. Kneeling, he pushed the raft off the bank side and away from the shallows. Amanda was scooping water, trying to row with her hands on one side of the raft. Jonathan jumped to his feet as best he could, and pushed the raft off with the flexible pole.

William overenthusiastically pushed hard again from the same side.

"Willie! Alternate sides!" yelled Jonathan. "We're going round in circles!"

Sure enough, they were now facing the ghoulish figure, which had begun to crawl towards them again, its grotesquely disfigured gray-green face dipping in and out of the water, and its disconnected eyeball bobbing along on the surface of the river.

"Shit! Shit! Oh, shit!" cried Amanda, splashing up scoops of water in a feeble attempt to propel the raft away, as the boys quickly resolved their steering issues and pushed together away from the fiendish corpse that steadily made its grim way towards them.

"Christ! What the hell?" Amanda gasped, once they were making some headway from the bobbing gray head, increasing their lead.

"Ghouls. Zombies," muttered Jonathan.

"From the asylum?" Amanda wondered, picturing dozens of the creatures following their trail from the hospital, throwing themselves in the river upstream, making their haggard way after them, tumbling through the waters, bashed by felled tree branches, and feeling nothing.

"They could be from anywhere," Jonathan asserted. "Let's face it. Where did the asylum ones come from?"

They were still in the shallower waters, protected from the main current being funneled through the gap in the bridge, making dangerous whitewater rushes filled with lumber, branches and mangled ironwork.

Amanda stared helplessly at the bobbing figure, still determined to follow them. "What do we do?"

"Get away!" Jonathan responded simply.

"Tell me, seriously," she persisted. "Can we kill them? If so, how?"

"Cut their heads off," Jonathan persisted. "Otherwise, we can delay them, but we can't stop them."

"Great," Amanda said, through gritted teeth. "It's like we've really got a few axes with us. And a guillotine."

"Who's sarcastic now?" Jonathan allowed himself a wry smile, and breathed easy, watching the gray bobbing head becoming more distant.

A sudden jerk downwards on the raft made Jonathan lose his footing, and he staggered towards the dark waters lapping at the edge of the raft, held back only by William lunging for the back of his belt.

"What the hell?" Jonathan said, peering down into the water between the bobbing white water container and the light metal can that William had lashed to the side of the raft.

With a sudden splash, a gray splayed hand – followed by a skinny stick of an arm – rose up out of the river and grasped the end of one of the boards. Another gnarled hand joined it and commenced to tug down at the raft, dipping one corner into the dark waters.

Jonathan responded by stamping hard with his winter boot on one hand and stabbing down hard with the broken end of his pole on the other. Meanwhile, William and Amanda lurched over the other side of the raft to counterbalance it, and compensate for the tipping of the opposite corner.

Amanda's hair dipped into the river water as she strained over the side of the raft.

"Ow!" she yelled, her head still down towards the water.

An icy hand had risen from the depths and entangled its bony fingers in the strands of her hair, grasping a full handful. Before she realized it, Amanda's hair was wound tight round its fist, as it pulled her head down into the depths.

William held Amanda around the waist with one hand, while lashing wildly at the hand with the two-by-four with the other so close to Amanda's head that she didn't know which was worse – being clubbed to death by her nephew, or drowned by a faceless ghoul!

She dug her nails into the leathery fingers of the ghoul beneath the waterline, prising her own fingers around its knobby fingers. Her head dipped into the water and she opened her eyes.

Through the murky depths she saw the hideous remains of a face, rags of skin floating eerily off torn gray flesh, and the exposed dirty white bones of its skull. The horror had no eyes, yet opened its grinning, fleshless lips in a hideous gape!

Amanda prised open the skeletal fingers and violently tugged her head sharply out of the water, and gasped in air, sensing her hair rip from her head with the sudden strong force she'd exerted, determined to release herself from the ghoul's death-grip. She didn't care if she'd been scalped – as long as she was free.

But the ghoul kept hold of one of her hands, grasping her two longest fingers so tightly she thought they might be ripped off. *Better that, than her being pulled into the waters at the ghoul's mercy!* Amanda thought.

By this time, Jonathan had pushed William to one side, grabbing the two-by-four from his hand and lending the endeavors some brute, masculine strength. William was still just a boy after all and Jonathan instinctively wanted to protect and save Amanda. William was able to hold Amanda onto the makeshift raft now with both his arms, so he was still doing all he could to help her.

Jonathan lashed out at the bony arm with the thick length of wood, being careful to avoid Amanda's hand.

Amanda, still gasping for breath after her moments underwater, said, "Hit it! I don't care if you break my hand! Just get it off me!"

Jonathan couldn't bring himself to hammer on her fingers and hesitated.

In that moment, the half-skinned skull rose out of the waters, the black empty sockets of its eyes gushing waterfalls of river water, and the gray flesh and skin of half its face peeling off like a rotten corpse. It opened its ghastly exposed jawbones to take a bite at Amanda.

Jonathan struck. He swung the length of two-by-four like a baseball bat and swept the head from its bony neck, so that it flew through the air and landed in the water some yards away with a soft splash.

The bony hand immediately released its grasp of Amanda's hand and sank without trace. Amanda sat back on middle of the raft, shaking her hand back to life, her body trembling.

In their devotion to saving Amanda, all of Jonathan and William's concentration had focused on keeping her on board and killing the ghoul that had a hold of her.

Behind them, however, they had been entirely unaware of another ghoul clambering its ragged corpse onto the other side of the swiftly moving raft.

Amanda looked up and shouted, "Willie, look out!"

The ghoul fell upon William, scrabbling at his throat in order to uncover a throbbing vein that it could feast upon. It opened its broken lips, revealing jagged teeth, and slavered in anticipation, red eyes gleaming.

Jonathan was tugging it off the boy's body, wrenching at its shoulders to buy some time. He grasped at its head, wondering if he could literally rip off its head with his bare hands, but this one was not as decomposed as the other, and it had superhuman strength for its current dead state.

Jonathan couldn't reach back to take a swing at this ghoul, since he dared not stop pulling it away from the vulnerable William. It would only take a split second for its fangs to sink into Willie's warm vein, and he would be dead. Jonathan couldn't take the risk of that happening. Maybe he could just get a good grip and at least break its neck. Then he could see about decapitating it. It just needed to be separated from its body. That's all.

For now, Jonathan struggled to delay the ghoul's onslaught, while the beast had already overpowered William who lay on his back, powerless as the monster knelt over him, weighing him down.

The creature appeared unfazed by Jonathan, who gripped its head and shoulders, and was barely held back from his grim intent. It was as if Jonathan was an annoying mosquito. Despite Jonathan using all his strength to attempt to wrench the creature off the boy, the ghoul barely noticed. William's own flailing hands were ignored as the ghoul persisted in his cruel intent. It ripped at William's jacket and shirt, exposing his neck and…

"Haaaaaa!" the creature recoiled suddenly and hissed, holding up its hands, and lurching back on its haunches.

William's crucifix, which he wore on a chain round his neck, had slipped into view with the ghoul's scrabbling.

In the moment that the creature sat back in horror at the holy symbol, Amanda punched the ghoul square in its rotting face. A huge blue energy blast flew out of her hand, which blinded all of them, and the ghoul was blasted way off the boat, its head flying off from its body.

"What the hell…?" said Jonathan once again, wide-eyed.

Amanda looked at her fist, and into Jonathan's eyes, a terrified look in her own. "What did I do?" she implored, seeking answers from the vampire hunter.

"You tell *me*," Jonathan said, raising his eyebrows, glancing into the distance in the direction the corpse had flown.

"Jesus!" shouted Amanda.

"Yes, it was probably the Lord," nodded William, sitting upright and adjusting his clothes against the weather. "Christ the Lord!" he yelled, and pointed.

The silvery fingers of another ghostly gray hand were reaching over the edge of a board.

"How many of them are there?" roared Jonathan, smashing off the fingers with one harsh blow of the two-by-four. Mashed green flesh and splintered bone edged the raft.

"Oh! More in the distance!" Amanda squealed.

"Let's get out of here!" yelled Jonathan.

Since they were far enough away from both the tremendous bottleneck gush from the broken gap in the bridge and the flying debris that could also endanger their lives, Jonathan pushed the raft into the faster-flowing midstream.

They witnessed several ragged corpses a good ways from them. Some were lying still as logs while others raised sinister gray limbs towards them in a lethargic attempt to drive themselves closer to the escaping raft.

The trio wasted no time. They paddled the best they could and that effort combined with the rapid flow of the swollen river drove them further away from the ghouls.

They heard a tremendous groaning sound that made them all look at one another in alarm. This was followed by a loud crack like a thunderclap.

"What's that?" cried William.

Jonathan stared upstream, "The bridge. It can't take any more!"

"Neither can I!" shrieked Amanda. "What do we do now?"

"It's okay. I reckon we're safe this far away. It's not a tsunami, and if we keep ahead in the fastest stream, it won't catch up with us. It can't flow faster than the river. If anything comes near, we just punt ourselves out of the way of the worst debris."

"Punt?" asked William.

"Yeah, punt," said Jonathan. "Like the gondoliers in Venice, the English in Oxford take out a flatboat called a punt and push their way through the river with a pole."

"Jeez… so now we're in England? Then we were in Venice, Italy? We get around!" Amanda rolled her eyes.

"Certainly has been a trip of a lifetime," agreed Jonathan. "Hold onto your hats! And the raft!"

The force of the water behind them sent them speeding onward, down river, faster than ever before. The water containers bobbed and rattled beside them but did their job. Jonathan, William, and Amanda gripped the edges of the raft as if their lives depended on it.

They did.

The trio heard gargled, distant shrieks behind them high above the sound of rushing waters and crashing lumber.

"Let's hope it takes all the heads off them," muttered William.

Jonathan nodded. "Reckon they'll be smashed to pieces. That bridge sure was heavy, without all the junk that had built up behind it. It'll be like a road roller and harvester all rolled into one."

Their makeshift boat-raft moved swiftly downstream and away from the ghoulish attackers – or at least what remained of them after the torrents and heavy onslaught of twisted metal, trees and heavy pieces of trash that had accumulated for the past few hours buried them with the collapse of the bridge.

As the trio rode the rapid river flow, they concentrated on maintaining their balance and catching their breath after their ordeal. No one spoke, but each was caught up in his or her own thoughts.

Jonathan was puzzling over what had happened when Amanda had swung a punch at the ghoul attacking William. There was something troubling him – a memory that escaped him, or lay beyond reach. And then there was what he thought he had seen.

From the corner of his eye, although almost blinded by the flash of blue light that appeared to burst from Amanda's hand, he thought he had seen something else.

Just for the second it had taken for her hand to strike the ghoul and blast him through the air, Jonathan thought he had caught sight of something ghostly and ethereal behind Amanda's back. No, not really *behind* her back, but *on* her back, attached to her back. In fact, they seemed to be part of her back.

Jonathan couldn't be sure, but he thought he had seen wings. Yes, great shimmering translucent wings. *That was crazy, wasn't it?* he thought. *No more crazy than the rest of his life had been.*

And then Jonathan remembered where he had seen something like that before. A woman surrounded by a pale blue aura; a woman with wings, usually concealed, yet released at specific moments.

It reminded Jonathan of his encounter with the Asian masseuse, Tina, five years ago. The old lady had told him that they were faes. So… that meant… Could Amanda be a fae?

He looked at Amanda, sitting with her hands clasped on her bent knees, her chin resting on her hands. The wind was blowing her hair dry, and she sat enjoying the breeze and the freedom.

She was oblivious to what she'd done. If she was a fae, Jonathan was pretty sure she didn't know, and had no idea what that meant.

For her part, Amanda had spent time wondering what had happened. *It must just be the way of ghouls*, she decided. *If you caught them square on the face, maybe that's just what happened to them.* But that didn't explain the surge of power she had felt just before she hit him.

CHAPTER 8

There was rarely a day when Rebecca Holbert would come to work at the Tarklin Roadside Café that she did not think about her sister Samantha. One evening over three years ago, Sam started her shift at the diner and simply disappeared. A massive search immediately followed, but to this day, the whereabouts of Samantha remained a mystery.

Like many small-town diners, the Café was typically staffed with two waitresses at minimum and a short-order cook. The cook was their dad, Parker Holbert, or Parke for short. That fateful night, Rebecca was very sick with the flu and worrying customers with her extended coughing spells and runny nose. Parke decided it best to leave work and take her to see Dr. Seward over in Melas and get her some antibiotics.

"I'll be right back, Sammie," Parke had told his one daughter as he departed. "Hold down the fort till we get back, okay?"

"No problem, Pops," she had told him. "Everyone's getting the 'special' until you get back."

That was the last time Parke had ever spoken to her.

When Parke and Rebecca returned from the clinic, a police car was parked outside and an officer was sitting at a table waiting to be served. He advised them that he had been there for over an hour to pick up some food for the night patrol and thought it suspicious that the diner was left unattended.

That started the Café's dark period and neither of the two would ever be the same.

Every day since then, Parke and Rebecca would come to work and quietly hope to see Sammie come back to the family business. Unfortunately, that never happened.

The holidays were especially difficult for the Holberts with their relative missing and now, three years later, it was no different. On the outside, they tried to appear jovial and in the Christmas spirit, but both were still very torn up at the unsolved mystery.

But, like most small business owners, the family buckled down and continued on. Tonight would be busy. The Café had a Christmas Eve buffet and patrons had started showing up early in the afternoon.

Unfortunately, the Café was not as festive as usual because all of the customers had their full attention tuned in to the breaking news happening over at the Dark Hollow Mine. Almost fifty workers had been trapped and ever-growing floodwaters were becoming a grave concern for the rescue workers.

In the small community of Tarklin, most of the folks either had family that worked in the mine or knew someone who was there. Some of the day shift workers from that very mine were in the diner solemnly watching the news with the rest of the customers.

The customers were talking about some of the "newbies" down in the mine covering the night shift. One of them was Ben "Bubba" Boyer. Rebecca went to school with Ben, though she was probably one of the few that called him by his real name. She prayed that Ben and the rest of the miners down in Dark Hollow would be okay.

At around 8:30 p.m., the rain started picking up again. Dave Snipe came through the doors of the Café and looked like a drowned cat as he made his way to the counter bar.

"Hey Becky, gimme the usual!" he called out.

"Hi Dave. There's a buffet tonight, so go on up and help yourself. I'll grab you some coffee."

Cyrus Rose, an off-duty deputy, was also sitting at the bar. He had been gravely watching the news of the miners unfolding on the TV and minding his time at the Café. He figured that any time now, he would be called to report for duty.

"Dave," Cyrus announced, "you look like you swam here! How's the mill?"

Dave Snipe owned a sawmill not too far from there and the two men went way back as friends. "Rosie, it ain't looking too good," Dave replied.

"Is the water in the lumberyard?"

"Yeah. About two feet. There are no workers, tonight being Christmas and all, so I just had to abandon the operation and head for higher ground."

"You are insured, right?"

"Of course – the bank says I'm in a flood zone. I've been paying for years on that policy and never had to make a claim. That might be changing after tonight."

"There's something unnatural going on!" an old woman called out from a nearby booth. "I heard it myself. Thunder in them hills and a rumbling down below!"

Cyrus shuddered but did not reply.

"Perhaps the mines are belching," Dave offered half-heartedly, like a joke.

"It ain't the mines," the old lady observed. "It's the *evil* I tell you! The evil is coming!" The way she pronounced "evil" reminded Cyrus of the voice of the Green Witch in the Wizard of Oz.

"Mrs. Muldrew, stop scaring the customers!" Rebecca called out in a lighter humor, hoping to soften the climate. "We don't need any more worries added to what's going on with those miners."

"Missy – you just don't understand," Mrs. Muldrew replied. "These are weird and unnatural circumstances going on out there." She pointed to the window. It was pitch black and the only thing one could see through the window was the motion of water as it cascaded over the glass.

Mrs. Muldrew continued: "This afternoon, I lied down to take a nap and was suddenly awakened by a loud explosion followed by a rumbling noise not far from my house. I was badly frightened. This was then followed by a terrific downpour that sounded as if an enormous tank had opened at the bottom and all the water dumped out at once. That!" She pointed an arthritic finger towards the window at the rain coming down. "And it hasn't stopped since!"

Becky came over to top off her coffee. "Don't worry dear," Becky said. "You can stay nice and dry right here as long as you need to."

"It's more than the rain, Missy. There's *something* else. I just know it – I feel it in me bones!"

Dave looked over at his friend and whispered, "I think the lady may be nuts, but I can't say that I don't believe her. With the miner accident, the flooding, and Melas over their being a ghost town – it's almost as if some great darkness is sweeping the land like a cancer and we're just now starting to feel its effects."

On the television screen, cameras showed the body of one of the miners being brought into the National Guard barracks in Melas.

"I'm beginning to think you're right," Cyrus Rose replied.

Unbeknownst to any of the patrons in the Tarlin Roadside Café that night, Mrs. Muldrew was not too far off in her prophetic observations. By 9:00 p.m., acres of area farmland were underwater and much of the fertile topsoil washed away. Every backwoods road had been turned into a creek. Every mountain stream was now on a rampage. The very earth itself could not absorb any more water and it was at this point that water began flowing over the top of the dam at Floyd Lake just a few miles upstream from where the group sat at the diner.

CHAPTER 9

"Shit and Shinola!" Henry Cane muttered, hunched over the steering wheel of the Hummer, peering through the windshield. "Fucking storm! First snow and now I can hardly see through this rain."

The wipers whipped back and forth, but the downpour was so great that they had hardly swept any water away before the following torrents obscured Cane's view.

"You'll thank the rain if things work out the way I planned," grinned Talman.

"You? Plan? That sounds ominous. All I need is for you to have another fucking plan. As if things aren't bad enough!"

He swung the wheel crazily as the Hummer hydroplaned through a deep flowing puddle – more like a creek – which ran across the road. His knuckles were white as he gripped the wheel to regain control.

"Henry, just drive. Fast as you can!"

"I am!" snarled the Doctor, his glasses steaming up with sweat. "We've only got till dawn to get Ralphie's body and reverse the exorcism!"

They travelled south down Interstate 79, and then east on Route 33 until they approached the Weston Bridge crossing the swollen West Fork River.

"Crap! River water's practically lapping over the bridge road!" said Talman.

The Hummer forded through the water, flood rain indistinguishable from the river already, and momentarily both men held their breath. Partway over the bridge, they truly thought that the force of the river would carry them away.

They were in the middle of gray, rapidly flowing water and Henry pressed the pedal to the metal, feeling the vehicle slide to the extent that he had the horrible sensation that they were floating off in the direction of downstream.

Talman sat further forward, teeth gritted, as if he could somehow move the car faster by doing so.

Just as they hit the far side of the river road, there was a bone-shattering crack and a middle section of the bridge behind them slowly creaked and dislodged, the metal tearing away from its supports.

Talman had wound down his car window and peered out behind him, "Fuckin'-A, Henry!"

The brothers had made it across the river before it collapsed.

"Shut up and let me concentrate!" yelled Henry. "I've got worse things on my mind to bother with than some shitty bridge!" Almost as an afterthought, he mumbled below his breath, "Hell, it needed replacing anyway."

"Ah, just concentrate on driving, and stop worrying." Talman almost laughed, half-mocking his brother.

"Fuck off!" Henry snarled. "This could be the end for us! Legion will not tolerate this! And you find it so funny?"

Talman sat with his arms folded in satisfaction, his mouth shut, smirking.

"I don't believe your attitude, you idiot." Henry shook his head.

Talman turned to him and gave an eerie, slow smile. "Believe me, brother. You have nothing to worry about. Thanks to me, all your troubles will be washed away!"

Henry glanced at him and ground his teeth together to prevent himself from lashing out at the grinning fool in fury and frustration. He wasn't interested in playing Talman's stupid guessing games, and refused to be drawn into his brother's attempts to bait him into asking pointless questions.

He had better and more important things to think about. Even if they made it back to the asylum before the first light of dawn, there was the fae to contend with. He could only hope that this bloody rain would release the snowbound cars and not freeze them in further. With any luck, the fae would have left by now. Henry Cane just wasn't sure how much luck he had left in this world.

Talman turned to his brother, and, as if reading his mind, said, "And if this fae is still around, this time, we offer no mercy. This time we kill her outright!"

Henry flicked a glance towards his infuriatingly grinning passenger, but remained silent in his assent.

He swung into the driveway of the asylum. The top powdery layers of snow had been washed away by the rain, so the Hummer took the compacted ice on the roadway with ease, just the occasional helpless glide onto the indiscernible lawn preventing them from driving swiftly and directly to the front door.

***

A handful of distraught staff stood at the entrance, debating between running to escape, and tending to the few remaining patients who were left alive in the asylum after the ghastly events of the night. All the ghouls who had attacked within the building seemed to have either fled during the exorcism or been staked or decapitated in the battle. It had taken some time before the stunned and fearful few left alive had crept from their hiding places to congregate in the hallway. A small number of patients remained asleep or locked in their rooms, unaware of the terrible fate of the other residents.

"Thank God!" cried one of the orderlies upon seeing the determined figure of Dr. Henry Cane appearing through the dark and the sleet. Cane smiled at the irony of the phrase. It was not God that the man had to thank for Henry's appearance. Quite the opposite.

"Dr. Cane! The phones are down and for some reason, none of us can get a signal on our cells to call for help!"

Good! thought Henry, barging through the weeping, shocked handful of staff crowding the doorway, Talman beside him.

111

"Nobody move. No one leave. I'll handle this now," commanded Henry Cane, turning his steely glare upon the staff.

"Where are those visitors? Dead?" Henry asked hopefully.

"The policemen are," said an orderly, "but we ain't seen the others a while. Mebbees gone."

Hmm, thought Henry, *Amanda Davenport the fae and the two others – a man and a teenager – gone. That made things a hell of a lot easier.*

"Contain the patients in the rec hall," the doctor said briskly, taking command. "Yes, even those in confinement already. It is vital that everyone stays together. Collect those who are left, and bring them all to the rec, while I attend to the small boy."

"He's dead, Doctor!" said a nurse.

"All the same. I have to check, since he has a history of catalepsy."

The nurse frowned. She was an experienced nurse, and had checked the boy herself. There was no way he was merely unconscious or asleep. He had no vital signs! Yet she didn't dare argue with this senior doctor.

"If he is dead, I must complete the death certificate," Henry added, immediately regretting it, for the nurse looked even more curiously at him. With so many patients and staff dead, why would he be so eager to examine one boy?

"Attend to the living, nurse!" Henry ordered, and she hurried off to help her colleagues round up the remaining patients.

Henry and Talman burst into the room in which Ralphie's body lay pale and motionless in his mother's arms. Cathy looked up, her face still puffy and red from crying, but resigned. Henry rushed over to Ralphie's body to examine it. Since Ralphie was a vampire at the time of the exorcism, the "true death" was not complete until a stake was driven through his heart, he was decapitated, or exposed to the sunlight.

Clearly, none of these were the case, and Henry's stony heart thrilled with excitement. He salivated with delight, unable to believe his good fortune, and gave a most uncharacteristic grin up to his brother's enquiring eyes.

"He's perfect! Untouched!" Henry said, barely able to contain his relief and gratitude.

Cathy was stroking Ralphie's face and barely registered who had entered the room, but she muttered to anyone who would hear, "I thought I had him back!"

Henry's eyes gleamed, "And so you shall!"

Cathy lifted her exhausted, swollen face up to Henry, and looked at him with blank eyes, veiled in grief.

"Not in front of her, though, Henry," warned Talman.

"Easily remedied!" Henry took hold of Cathy's forehead with one hand, and she fell back in a dead faint. "OK! Now we reverse the exorcism, and bring Legion back into Ralphie's body. Swiftly and before dawn!"

Talman quickly pulled a stick of chalk out from his pocket and began to draw a circle around himself and Henry.

"If only we had time to take him to the obelisk," complained Talman. "At least we know that it was tied to Legion, and guaranteed success!"

Unwilling to concede any doubt of summoning back Legion, Henry ignored this comment to rummage in his own pocket, and pulled out some items. He lit a black candle with a lighter and sprinkled some herbs over the lit flame, so that they crackled and fizzed.

"Are you ready?" he asked Talman, grim-faced.

Talman stepped into the circle, and made a gesture with his hand as if he were addressing an audience, giving Henry the floor.

"O, Father Lucifer and Demon Legion!" Henry intoned, his arms raised as he and his brother stood within the circle.

"We entreat you! By the virtue of the evil resurrection, and the torments of the damned, I conjure and exorcise thee, Spirits of Ralphie Edwards deceased and Legion eternal, to answer my liege demands, being obedient unto these sacred ceremonies, on pain of everlasting torment and distress... Berald, Beroald, Balbin! Gab, Gabor, Agaba! Arise, arise, I charge and command thee!"

For a second, nothing happened, and Talman and Henry looked nervously at each another. The dark night sky was lightening outside, and dawn would break shortly. Henry's desperate face was dripping with sweat.

Unknown to them, a huge white bat, shimmering in the darkness outside in the last of the night sky, winged its way towards the asylum. Its swift, leathery wings cut through the night like a well-honed sword, and it wheeled over the building, soaring lower, before it alighted on the tiled roof without a sound.

Simultaneously, a vapor of white gas swirled from the ceiling of the room, and entered Ralphie's mouth.

Henry gasped in relief, clutching his brother's arm.

"It's worked!" Talman murmured softly.

"How could you doubt Legion?" Henry scoffed, regaining his arrogance now.

Ralphie took in a small breath that engulfed the whole cloud of vapor, then his body convulsed as if it was in ecstasy.

Henry and Talman stood entranced, watching the transformation and waiting for the boy's small body to become fully possessed by the powerful demon, as before. Henry braced himself for the strong, loud and commanding tones of the demon Legion to give him the sort of abusive tongue-lashing he expected because of so many things not going to plan. His wrath would be awful!

Ralphie sat up abruptly, and Henry and Talman jerked back in shock, awaiting their torrid eardrum-busting lecture from the disgruntled demon.

Ralphie's little freckled face gave a wide, sinister smile, "Well gentlemen," said a steady, controlled masculine voice, "so, you have brought me here to Earth!"

"Again!" grinned Talman, and Henry jabbed him sharply in the ribs.

Ralphie's eyes gleamed red, the eerie smile still fixed on his face. "Clever little cambions," he said quietly.

Henry and Talman exchanged glances. This was not the outraged, powerful Legion they knew, and they were unnerved by his reaction, waiting for the strike out of the blue. Above all, they knew not to trust a demon, especially not one so high in the hierarchy of the damned, such as Legion. He could turn against them at any moment. But this calm, simmering malevolence was something else, something more fearsome than his usual loud brashness – it was like a change of personality, and it scared the Canes. Henry bolstered himself up, putting on a front of arrogance to conceal the anxiety he felt deep within.

"So," the voice said, through Ralphie, raising the volume slightly, "what shall we do now?"

Talman gulped, but Henry answered clearly, stepping confidently out of the magic circle and facing Ralphie's stare brazenly.

"We get rid of the witnesses!" the Doctor announced.

Talman clapped his hands in delight. "Kill them all!"

"Wait," interjected Henry. "Although it is only right, and we are fit to massacre the remaining staff and patients, I suggest we rebuild our vampire army instead."

"You suggest well, Henry Cane," the voice, now Ralphie's own childish voice box, said. "And bring me their blood to feast upon!" His eyes glowed red again, and he bared his baby teeth – long canines and incisor teeth sliding outside his lips before their very eyes.

"Indeed, Legion!" Henry bowed sharply.

Ralphie gave a chuckling, childish hysterical laugh that went on for some seconds, leaving Henry and Talman bewildered. They set off for the door.

"Don't be long, now!" Ralphie said in a singsong voice, "I'm very, very thirsty. If you take too long, I might have to drain 'Mommy'!" He nodded towards the unconscious figure of Cathy Edwards, lying beside him, "And that would be so-o-o sad!" His little face puckered into a mask of infantile despair, and then he roared with laughter, which echoed after the two Crane brothers as they exited the door.

"What's with him?" Talman said, nodding his head sideways towards the room they'd just left.

"I don't know. But I don't like it," Henry asserted grimly, heading for the rec room.

"Wow! He must be so mad to be behaving like this!"

"That's what worries me."

Henry had expected fire, brimstone, and fury from Legion because the Canes had let him down again, leaving him to be banished by an inexperienced priest; but Henry had not anticipated this quiet, contained evil, and sneering mockery, which was so much more terrifying than his blatant hell-mongering. Henry could only wonder what terrible outburst or punishment awaited them when Legion was done toying with them.

Henry swung the door into the rec hall, where the handful of quavering staff had rounded up a dozen remaining patients. They sat huddled in a group around two tables at the edge of the dance floor. The blow-up Santa, twinkling tree, garish Christmas decorations, and balloons looked oddly incongruous in the face of

117

all the death and destruction that had gone on in the rest of the building.

Three patients were heavily drugged and in straightjackets, sitting slumped where they had been placed. Many of the staff wished they could be pharmaceutically "out of it" too.

The alert staff and the more conscious patients looked up in alarm as the door swung open. Their concern changed to relief and hope when they saw the familiar doctor and his brother, Talman. Or as they thought – Josef McClumpy from the funeral home in Tarklin.

The onlookers weren't even surprised to see a funeral director here, now. After all, there were hundreds of dead bodies that needed moving at some point. Although God knows, it didn't seem a priority at this point in time.

But most of their hope and trust lay in their glorious leader, Dr. Henry Cane.

How misplaced was their judgment!

Talman held back, waiting to see how Henry was going to play the situation. He had received no instructions from his brother and wondered how they would effect the transformation of this group without instilling panic and violent battle. There were only two of them, after all – and Legion, who was still in a delicate stage of transition into the body of Ralphie. His power and strength would grow with each suck of blood he consumed.

Henry approached the cluster of people and spoke calmly: "Here's what we'll do, folks. The danger appears to be over, but we need to be vigilant at all times. Evacuation at a slow and gradual pace. We wish to escort you, in pairs, to safety."

The eighteen or so avid listeners started muttering amongst themselves.

The muttering increased, with some discernible phrases: "Yeah – I don't wanna be left here!" and "Slow evacuation? What the hell!"

Henry called for order, and continued, "In pairs – or in the case of the more serious cases – one patient accompanied by two members of staff. We will lead you safely to one of the cars outside, where you will be driven into town to a place where you will be comfortable and safe!"

"What about the ambulance?" said a nurse. "We could all travel together in one of those! Why don't we all go at once!?"

The muttering increased again as people questioned the proposition. They didn't realize that they had no choice.

Henry Cane held up his hands for silence, which fell instantly. In times of chaos and emergency, people look for leadership, and they had found it in the serious, bespectacled psychiatrist before them.

"The ambulance has been destroyed. Do not question my logic, but trust! It is your only solution!"

Talman nodded authoritatively, since it was the only thing he could think of to do, apart from kill them where they stood or drag them bodily to Legion to be sucked into vampirism. Henry was the clever, subtle one, and Talman would take his lead from him.

"Okay." Henry clapped his hands together. "First two: you and you!" He pointed to two of the stronger patients. "Come with us. The rest of you: it is imperative that you stay where you are. There is strength in numbers. We won't be long and you will all be safe here."

Talman and Henry led the two patients out the door and turned left towards the wing where Ralphie sat waiting.

"Aren't we going out the front?" asked one of the patients, Toni Butcher, who was due to be discharged the following week. Toni was a muscular black woman in her mid-thirties that towered a good foot over the other patient, a timid man called Trent. Trent said nothing. Doctor knew best, after all.

"No. This exit…" said Henry sternly, striding on, careful to ensure that the patients kept pace.

They arrived at Cathy's room and Toni frowned. "This isn't right!" she cried, as Henry pushed open the door.

Henry squeezed Toni's shoulder and her legs buckled. Just as she was about to scream, he clamped a hand over her mouth and pushed her full into the room.

Trent stood bewildered. Suddently, Talman shoved him into the room too.

Cathy was sitting up on her bed, delirious with delight at seeing her small son miraculously alive and well, smoothing Ralphie's hair and cooing endearments in his ear.

Toni's brow furrowed with puzzlement at the intimate and domestic scene before her: Cathy and her cute cherubic son. So why had they come here?

"Legion!" said Henry, his hand still clasped over Toni's mouth.

Ralphie chuckled a childish laugh. "Oh, that tickles me!" he said, in Ralphie's sweet voice.

"The choice is yours – this one is spunky," said Henry. "This one…" he cocked his head towards Trent, frozen in surprise beside him, "this one is feeble!"

"Spunky! Spunky!" Ralphie jumped up and down on the bed in childish delight, then bounded onto the floor and ran over to Toni.

Henry, still holding Toni tightly across the mouth and around her middle, bent her at the waist down towards Ralphie's face.

Ralphie's eyes gleamed red and his voice deepened into that of the demon as he said, "Give me spunky every time!"

He opened his mouth, exposing razor-sharp canines, and sank his teeth into Toni's throat with a crunch.

Cathy gazed unseeingly at her beloved son, as if blinded by grief and sudden joy – sent mad by extremes of emotion. She sang nursery rhymes and gazed into the mid-distance.

Loud slurping sounds broke timid Trent's silence and he started whimpering tiny, tiny, sounds. Talman stepped forward and held his arms in case he made his escape. Then Trent wet himself and fainted.

"See!" said Henry in disgust, "I told you – feeble!"

"Shit!" cried Talman, releasing his hold on Trent's arms and letting him drop into his own puddle of urine. "Loser's pissed on my shoes!"

***

The staff were the worst – even more questioning of Cane's wisdom and authority than Toni Butcher had been. On more than one occasion, Henry or Talman had to deliver a swift backhander or karate chop to the carotid to immobilize them or knock them unconscious.

Henry shook his head with disgust – that was such a bother! They usually had to knock out the other one before they freaked, and then drag their sorry asses down the corridors and through the wing to Cathy's room. *Much better for them to walk to Ralphie under their own steam*, he thought.

They gave Ralphie – or Legion – the choice of who to kill outright, draining them of all blood, and who to bite, suck, and to take to the brink of death. This meant the difference between death and eternal living death as a vampire.

Ralphie was very thirsty and hungered for fresh flesh and blood. Sometimes he forgot to stop, so enjoying the gush of warm, metallic strength that flooded his mouth and flowed so easily down his parched throat.

Twice he sucked overly hard and long, non-stop until the body was drained dry. Twice he was so over-enthusiastic that he completely mashed the carotid artery and the flesh around it with his voracious teeth, and munched at the throat until it was a red mush, useless and incompatible with life. Four times, therefore, he found himself with a completely dead body on his hands.

"Oops!" he said, in his little-boy voice, pointing an innocent forefinger to his bloody lips, and Henry and

Talman were left to dispose of the body for fear that one of the survivors would see it and panic. "As if there weren't enough bodies lying around!" Henry scoffed.

"The exuberance of youth!" replied Ralphie as he shrugged his little boy shoulders apologetically and smiled a bloody smile.

The others he sucked until he felt their pulse weaken, and then he stopped. Strictly speaking, only a small bite and the transmission of his saliva into their bloodstream would convey eternal life – or living death, which was more accurate. But Ralphie needed blood. He would take as much as he could. It had been so long since new vampires had been created! Henry and Talman knew that they were witnessing a great thing.

The living dead, once they had recovered for a moment, were able to walk obediently away out of sight in another room to await instruction.

Two by two, the trusting survivors followed Henry and Talman Cane to their deaths. Each new death brought greater strength into Ralphie, who drank the blood greedily.

Whether they died completely – sucked to death or became the living dead – it was all the same. Their souls had died and gone to hell. Once their spirits escaped their bodies, they became imbued with demonic power and were transformed into vampires, emerging from death with a whole new personality and sense of purpose.

Ralphie sat back, the lower part of his face completely caked in blood. He rubbed his bloated child-tummy, and belched. A bubble of blood frothed from his mouth and he chuckled a Ralphie-laugh again.

Then he roared, "Any more?"

"These are the last," Talman said, undoing the straightjacket on the last of the new vampires before he joined his fellow undead in the next rooms.

"Oh, I don't think so!" the demonic voice said, eyes gleaming red, with a mischievous look from Talman to Henry.

Holy shit! thought Talman. *Does he mean us?*

Ralphie turned his head towards Cathy, still on the bed singing softly to herself, as if her system had shut down to protect what remained of her sanity.

Henry graciously wafted his hand slowly towards Cathy, as if offering her, saying, "Go ahead!"

This was a great sign, Henry concluded. If Ralphie was thinking of killing his mother, it meant that all vestiges of the little Ralphie Edwards were gone. Legion must be complete! Previously, the body of Ralphie had been propelled in part by a childish desire to see his mother. That's what had brought him here: that remaining tiny degree of humanity. And now – this! Cathy was as dispensable to him as an anonymous mental patient. Success indeed!

"And so, you would offer up the life of a child's mother without a thought?" the demon-voice mocked.

Henry's smile disappeared. *Was this a test?*

"Good man!" the demon laughed, approvingly, and both Talman and Henry breathed a sigh of relief.

Ralphie waddled over to Cathy's bedside, where he whispered, "Goodnight, Mommy" and kissed her throat.

He sank his teeth in momentarily, and she sighed. He withdrew.

"I don't like to see you looking pale, Mommy!" he grinned.

He turned around, wiping his bloody mouth on his sleeve, and addressed the stares of Henry and Talman Cane: "I suggest we leave the vampires here. They have intelligence enough to make a decent pretense at life. They might fool some people. And they will be ready for action when The End Times come, which will be soon!"

Henry frowned at this speech. Surely it was for Henry to say what happened next. He was in charge of The End Times here on earth. He felt usurped.

Ralphie continued gaily, "Well, gentlemen, and so to business!"

***

From the level of conversation in the Hummer, as Henry drove Talman and Ralphie away from the asylum, the "new" Ralphie had emerged with an extremely high adult level of intelligence and even greater demonic power.

Henry said little, but his mind was working overtime. Now that they had reached this stage, and now that Legion appeared to be at his full powers after so long, Henry was hell-bent on proceeding with The End Times. He had been so close in the 1940s, only to be thwarted. Now was his chance to act fast and effectively. And if he didn't act soon, the chance would be lost again.

Like the perfect storm, all elements were aligning themselves for success. Except Henry felt a tingle of jealousy where Legion was concerned. The End Times was Henry's project, and yet this demon was speaking with such knowledge and authority about it, that Henry feared for his life's work. They had made a great start, but more was to come.

The rains had slowed to a gentle shower, but the damage had been done to the environment. Knowing that bridges were down, Henry took U.S. Route 33 west from the asylum, then took back roads that were awash with mud. The sound of spray from the wheels was constant as the Hummer churned up puddles and forded through new creeks that had sprung up and ran suddenly across roads.

As if he could read Henry's mind, Ralphie spoke up from the back seat. "We have made a good start," intoned the demonic voice, "but there is much work to be done and long have I awaited this moment!"

Henry grunted agreement.

"We have almost all we need to exact the glorious End Times!" declared the demon.

Henry felt a prick of anger. It was Henry's to unleash, surely? He wanted the glory, the fame, the notoriety. Was it not fitting that a cambion – half demon, half human – should lead the opening of the Gateway to Hell in Melas? The portal between the worlds to be unlocked by one who bestrode those two worlds, was of two worlds?

Henry's father would surely have something to say if this demon Legion had ideas above his station. There would be the Devil himself to pay!

If the brothers were successful in killing off all the people in a town like Tarklin, there would be enough bloodshed to open the Gate, spilling forth the demonic realm into the real world.

The soil on the graves of the dead would rumple and crack as corpses rose to "life." But they would become undead zombies. Their gristly, dirt-caked figures would inspire widespread panic as they came out of the earth to roam and to kill. So many dead! They would be unstoppable! It would be impossible to exact the "true death" to overwhelming numbers.

There might be some casualties, it was true. Collateral damage, it was called. But it would take more than one human to behead every member of the undead, or to stake the hearts. The numbers alone would ensure certain victory!

Oh, it would be like the best days of World War II again! Henry almost chuckled at the remembrance of the heaps of corpses he had witnessed in concentration camps. The piles of bodies buried in trenches or incinerated. That was his triumph! Oh, the days of his manifestation as Heinrich Himmler had given him such a taste for The End Times, when evil reigned! And it could all happen again! Bigger, better and faster! The dead would rise again as the infernal damned on earth! Slain vampire spirits always manifested in the flesh once they escaped hell. The world would be theirs! What a glorious day!

Oh, Henry had lived for that moment! For over two hundred years, in many manifestations, taking many human forms, Henry had worked for this all his life. Only his foolish brother had worked with him tirelessly on this through the ages, and he knew his place, at least. But here was this demon, Legion, acting as if he knew it all!

Henry's dreams and visions of The End Times had given his life purpose and he wasn't about to give the project over to a demon he had summoned himself – no matter how powerful. Henry made a mental note to ensure that he controlled the demon and not the other way around.

Ralphie tapped Henry on the shoulder and brought him out of his contemplation. The demon's voice said frankly and without a note of sarcasm, "Just tell me what to do. You're the boss!"

Henry's eyes flickered to the rear-view mirror in surprise. Again, it was as if Legion knew what he was thinking. He shook his head. Coincidence, merely. Or maybe it was obvious that Henry was disgruntled and out of sorts.

Of course. That was it, Henry thought. He must make his feelings less plain. He'd had enough practice over the centuries. But now he was so close to achieving his lives-long dreams, perhaps he had let his emotions get the better of him. He straightened his face; straightened his mind; concentrated on driving.

Consequently, he didn't see through the rear-view mirror, the self-satisfied, mocking grin on Ralphie's face as he settled back in his seat and folded his chubby little arms in defiance.

CHAPTER 10

Jeff Abraham had been dead for nearly six hours by the time rescue workers found him. All of the miners had lost their lives on that fateful day when Bridge Creek filled the crevices of the darkened hollows below and into the ruptured mine shaft. Jeff, however, was the only body that was ever recovered.

As the ambulance carrying Jeff out of Dark Hollow Road crossed Bridge Creek, the State Police were quick to set up barricades blocking the road from anyone else entering Dark Hollow. The floodwaters had become too dangerous and within an hour later, had covered the bridge itself.

Unaware that Jeff would be the only person the county's emergency workers would recover, they set up a makeshift morgue and emergency staging area in nearby Melas, waiting uneasily for the waters to subside before returning to their rescue efforts.

This staging area was in the barracks of the West Virginia National Guard. Presently, the barracks looked vacant due to the Guard being dispatched to attend to unseasonal flooding throughout the state. One small crew of guardsmen stayed behind to man the barracks and another, led by the Captain, had just left to survey Bridge Creek and the Floyd Lake dam.

The body of Jeff Abraham was placed in a black body bag. As soon as authorities could reach his next of kin, they would make proper arrangements to have him sent to a funeral home.

***

It was just past 10:38 p.m. on Christmas Eve when Parke Holbert noticed water coming underneath the back door leading to the kitchen of the Tarklin Roadside Café. When he opened the door, he was confronted with a heavy, white mist-like-fog that was so thick he could not see more than a couple feet in front of him.

As unnerving as the mist was, what bothered Parke more was a terrible roaring sound coming from the north – from Melas. *What the heck?* Parke thought to himself.

The diner was slightly elevated, or else there would have been a lot more water coming into the establishment. The back door had a stoop and water was well over that and past the door seal.

Parke stepped out onto the porch and quickly closed the door behind him so as to prevent any more water from coming into the kitchen. He initially did not realize how deep the water had become, nor how it had surrounded the diner.

Without thinking, Parke stepped out into the mist, over the stoop, and submerged almost knee deep into the water that had surrounded the building. A small fence was behind the Café and Parke could not believe his eyes – the water was already nearing the top of the

130

fence posts! *Shit fire and save the matches! I better get back in and warn the others.*

As he tried to turn around and head back toward the Café, he suddenly became disoriented. He first thought that maybe the mist was playing visual tricks on him, but then he realized he was now waist-deep in the water and it was no longer a pool of water, but rather a raging current and he was being pulled downstream!

Somewhere in the flood debris, some barbed wire got washed away – probably from a fence upstream. This very wire snagged Parke's foot and before he knew it, he was being pulled deeper into the current and far away from the diner.

"Help!" he called out, but nobody heard him. Suddenly, he plunged full body into a whirlpool and deeper into the main body of Elk Creek. He was in a world of trouble now.

He struggled to regain control of the situation and to hopefully swim to shore. However, the more he tried to free himself from the barbed wire, the more entangled he became. Five minutes later, he drowned.

***

The effects of Talman Cane's "egg deposit" down the Floyd Lake drain four hours earlier had resulted in an implosion of the discharge pipe. By now, water at the dam had already started washing over the top – at the center, near where the catch basin used to function. It had taken no time for the current to wash across the crest of the dam and begin picking up pace.

Water had already covered the road at the foot of the dam and was a good foot deep there and the current was getting stronger every minute. In a very short time, the sheet of water spilling over the dam was a hundred yards wide and coming right over the middle.

At the main spillway, water roared over eight feet – like a miniature Niagara Falls.

By 9:30 p.m., several rocks on the outer face of the dam had washed away and the water jetting over the top had cut a hole into the face about twenty feet wide and six feet deep. As the unrelenting deluge kept pushing downwards into this hole, the dam's face kept crumbling away, little by little with each passing precious second.

At 9:45 p.m., the National Guard dispatched a boat up Bridge Creek to inspect the water levels at the dam. They immediately sent alerts out, but by now there was little anyone could do to stop what was about to happen.

After hearing the alerts, several more guardsmen showed up on the higher road accessing the dam and stood in rain-drenched awe in anticipation of what they were about to witness.

Captain Hanger – one of the soldiers on the banks of the lake that night – yelled, "Jefferson! Get the boat off the creek now! The dam's breaking. I repeat – the dam's breaking!"

"Yes sir," Jefferson reported from the other side of the radio.

The swiftly flowing torrent continued slicing at the dam's midsection little by little and then, all of the sudden, took out the dam in one mighty instant.

"Holy fuck!" Captain Hanger exclaimed.

When the dam let loose, Floyd Lake suddenly poured into the valley like a living being, hell-bent on the destruction of everything in its wake. By 10:36 p.m., the entire contents of Floyd Lake had been emptied.

Trees throughout the valley were snapped and uprooted. The hillsides on either end of the valley leading up to the dam were scraped bare. Every living thing had been washed out, leaving only bare rock and mud in its place. Downstream from Floyd Lake was Melas. Over the past twenty-four hours, water had been steadily pouring over the lake's dam, its water regulation system no longer able to keep up with the ever-increasing levels. When the dam broke, it sent a torrent of water gushing downstream. Downstream towards Melas.

The water advanced on the ghost town of Melas like a terrible wall. Huge chunks of the dam, fence posts, pieces of barns and houses, boulders, whole trees, and indescribable chunks of debris advanced this "wall" like large gears chewing everything – grinding everything in its path – advancing its ominous purpose. With each advance, the wall got higher and higher like a large hill rolling over and over.

The guardsmen at the dam looked at each other in astonishment.

"Status, Jefferson," Captain Hanger called out over the radio.

There was only silence.

The captain called the barracks in Melas and ordered an immediate evacuation of the remaining personnel. Although Melas was a ghost town for the most part, the few emergency service workers were immediately evacuated the moment they got word of the dam's collapse. This included evacuating the National Guard barracks, leaving behind everything including the lone body bag and its contents.

By the time the "wall of water" had reached the small bridge on the west side of Melas, it was almost sixty feet high and moving straight for the rear of the town at approximately twenty miles per hour. Pushing in front of it was an unconscionable amount of debris that was now comprised of acres of forest, several small bridges, scores of disintegrated houses, dead animals, raw sewage, and other things.

It was here that the aquatic monster took out the Methodist Church and pounced upon the emergency workers who had just moments before left the National Guard Barracks on their speedy retreat towards U.S. Route 50 and higher ground. In the misty dark, they did not see the wall of death until it was too late.

As water gushed through the town, it wasn't long before the makeshift mortuary flooded, taking the body bag downstream. Eventually it would wind up in Tarklin.

The flood smashed through downtown Melas like it was not even there. The historic caboose in the town square was obliterated almost instantly along with the now-vacant Dairy Queen, National Guard Barracks, the College Corner Restaurant, and several abandoned shops. The only structures that remained after the "wall" came through were the Melas Community College and Fort Melas, and these only survived because they were far way from Bridge Creek and the direct path of the flood.

The physical *matter* that used to be the town of Melas helped to slow down the overall velocity of the "wall" as it made its way to the next stop along its path: Tarklin. Unfortunately, the *matter* of Melas also significantly added to the unbelievable amount of debris already in the monster's belly.

Including the corpse of Jeff Abraham.

CHAPTER 11

At the Tarklin Roadside Café, Dave Snipe was onto his eighth cup of coffee by the time they heard the strange, deep rumbling sound close by, outside. Even through the persistent battering rain on the roof, everybody heard the loud, extended growling noise somewhere beyond the walls.

In that second, everyone stopped mid-bite, forks suspended in the air, ears intent and mouths open – and looked at one another in bewilderment. After a second of silence and wonder, as they strained their ears, trying to make sense of listening to the low, rolling rumble, a muttering chorus of such phrases as "What was that?" and "What the hell?" pervaded the crowded diner.

"Was that thunder?" Becky queried, staring wide-eyed at Dave, the coffee pot in her hand, poised over his cup where she had stopped pouring, mid-flow. *And where's Dad at?* she wondered. *He's been gone for a good while and the buffet is starting to look empty.*

"Strangest thunder crack I ever heard," off-duty Deputy Cyrus Rose frowned, ready to stand up and go to the door to investigate.

136

"Told you!" cried old Mrs. Muldrew. "I told you there was evil in the air! We're all doomed!"

"Hey lady, shut your hole!" yelled a truck driver unfamiliar to the place who'd only stopped for a bite to eat en route home and to take refuge from this shitty weather. He'd had enough of the old woman's babbling, since she'd been moaning on about wickedness and evil since he'd arrived thirty minutes ago – and probably before then! As if the stress of driving in this foul weather and his tiredness weren't enough, he was still 200 miles from home on Christmas Eve night and the old bag's shrill, strident voice and portents of doom were giving him a headache.

"Hey there," warned Cyrus, staring at the newcomer from beneath his threatening brows. He might be off-duty, but old Mrs. Muldrew was a long-established Tarklin resident, no matter how annoying, and Tarklin looked after its own.

"Fill me up when you're ready, Becky," Dave Snipe grunted, holding up his coffee cup as a reminder. Regardless of the strange sound outside and the curiosity of the other customers, he had a caffeine addiction to feed and he didn't care. He had enough troubles with his flooded sawmill and impending insurance claims. He hated paperwork.

Becky glanced at him distractedly, but took a few steps towards the window to see if she could make out what was happening. She still held the coffee pot delicately in one hand, cradling its hot belly with the other, padded with a cloth. Down in the coffee pot, the surface of the black liquid was gently shivering, making ripples. At first Becky couldn't tell if it was caused by her trembling or not, but when she looked up, the startled look on people's faces and the rattling of the cutlery and crockery told her that the whole diner was vibrating. Possibly the whole town. An earthquake?

Cyrus Rose had only crossed the diner and got halfway to the doorway when the world turned upside down, "Anybody know what...?"

A huge smashing and tearing sound drowned out his words, followed by splintering wood and metal, the rush of water, and suddenly – a cacophony of screams and shouts. The back wall of the kitchen seemed to fall forward on a wave of water, bringing with it the heavy cooking range and grill, smashing the wooden partition and pinning Dave Snipe under the counter.

His legs and torso were crushed. The top part of his body crumpled over the ground and his face fell into the cutlery cans, where he slowly bled from the mouth. Trickles of deep red blood flowed from his damaged internal organs, over his lips, and blossomed out into a diluted red, then flower of pink on the waterfall of river water that flowed over the counter.

No one had time to respond or to tend to his needs. Chaos ensued – everything happened within seconds, so that none of the occupants of the diner knew what had hit them, nor did they have time to prepare for the terrible events that were occurring.

At the same time the kitchen folded into the diner, several thick timbers – long lengths of tree trunks and logs from the flooded sawmills – shot through the thin walls of the diner, driven by the force of water on which they rode. They smashed into people and furniture as the walls crumpled and the roof collapsed. More shrieks of metal, creaks of wood, screams and moans from the customers rang out like a symphony of terror from inside.

The diner was quickly becoming a flooded tomb.

For once, the old woman said nothing: Mrs. Muldrew's wrinkled face was a mask of terror, her throat paralyzed with fear. Her eyes widened whitely and her thin-lipped mouth made a silent "O" shape, watching in horror as, cresting a wave of muddy water, the solid base of a lumberyard timber log came flying straight into her face, hurling her through the air and against the wall, smashing her dentures out through the back of her skull and killing her instantly.

Debris came flying through the air, either from outside on flumes of icy, rushing water or flung from the remains of the diner's building and contents. It smashed against the flimsy diner's construction, and the frail skin and bone of the humans who inhabited it.

Within seconds, the screams had strangely stopped, leaving the crash and creak of shifting timbers and building materials, and the torrents of water as the only sounds to be heard.

For the people caught in this disaster, all had gone black and silent. Minutes passed, nature taking its cruel course as the swollen river water – having broken the barrier in its way and deposited some of its heavier debris in the shattered diner – settled into more of a steady stream.

The counter where Dave Snipe had died was completely covered with sheet metal from the demolished wall. Only the white fingers of one hand hung beneath the wreckage to show where the body lay.

Somewhere beneath the roof were the battered bodies of Dave Snipe, who never did get his eighth cup of coffee; Mrs. Muldrew, the oracle of all evil, who never did get to boast of her premonitions; the visiting trucker, who never did get home, and the four other locals without family, who had stopped by in their loneliness to share their Christmas Eve and the special Tarklin Roadside Café buffet with their fellow townsfolk before midnight mass.

***

The first that Becky knew of her being still alive was the feel of her teeth chattering. She came to consciousness slowly, not knowing where she was; just knowing that she was terribly cold – icy cold, as if she was wet, too.

She opened her eyes, blinking her eyelashes into freezing water. She was lying in a pool of water! The rain was falling on her, so she must be outside, somehow.

She lifted her head, touching it on a piece of wood or something that she found out she was lying under.

She was shivering all over and drenched. More than that – there was glass, shattered all around her, mixed in with the water, and her back and cheek hurt. She lifted her hand and realized that she was still clutching the black plastic handle of the coffee pot, although no glass remained. But she was lying in more glass than a coffee pot could provide. *The plate glass window from the diner's front entrance*, she thought to herself. So that's where she was.

The pain in her back made her wince. With difficulty, she moved her hand to her face and touched where it hurt. She was so frozen cold and wet that she couldn't feel a thing. When she took her hand away from her cheek and looked at her fingers, she saw they were bloody. Goodness only knew what had happened, but she was pinned down by rubble, face first in a puddle of water, inside but somehow outside.

The place was eerily silent, except for the drumming rain and the sound of flowing water, but devoid of all signs of life – other than Becky, of course.

She groaned as she strained to move her legs beneath the broken table and piece of roof timber that covered her. She still lay on her stomach but scrabbled her feet, looking for some way to push herself out from under the mess that trapped her.

She dug her fingers into the pool of water, careless of the shards of glass, dragging herself slowly from the timber. It seemed impossible, and she felt so battered and exhausted, cold with exposure, that it would be easy to give up. Straining her painful back and crushed knee, she managed to inch her way a little, and then ease herself further up through the small gap.

She moved away some wood that barred her way with some difficulty, straining to push aside some heavy weights, until she was able to drag herself into a sitting position.

She sat up in the pool and raised her hands to rub the water and blood out of her eyes. She felt as if she'd been beaten up, every muscle aching, but she was glad to be alive.

What about Dad?

She looked around the demolished building from her seat on the ground, but could see little above the piles of debris and the driving rain. Her back hurt.

"Hello?" she cried, surprised at the weakness of her voice, so she cleared her throat and struggled to her feet, wobbling to balance herself with very little flat space beneath her feet.

Standing up, she became aware of the true extent of the damage. The place was destroyed! Where was her dad? She could hardly make out the orientation of the diner, from this mess. The roof – in shattered pieces – had fallen in and covered most of the floor space, and the walls had dropped into the sides. God knows whether anyone else had survived.

"Hello!" she shouted a bit louder, and strained her ears to listen above the rain and river. Was that a groan she heard? "Hello!" she repeated, and this time, she was sure.

To her left, towards where the front door had been, there was a definite moan or a cry for help. She clambered across the piles of building material and furniture, despite the pain in her back and the blood that poured from her face, desperate to find someone else alive.

"Hello! Where are you?" Becky yelled.

"Help," a small, weak cry emanated from beneath a pile of rubble.

Becky started shifting lengths of wood, her back stabbing her with agonizing knives. "I'm here! I'm coming!" she cried, motivated by hope and life. She dug with her bleeding fingers, pulling away lengths of sheeting and wood, until she made out a muddy hand and tousled hair. The head tilted up, gratefully. As soaked, cold and muddy as she was, there lay the desperate face of Deputy Cyrus Rose.

"What took you so long?" he gasped, and laughed with relief.

***

The body of Jeff Abraham, still in its black, zippered body bag, had made its undulating way downstream on a river of floodwater and come to a bumping stop against a dam of debris: trees and mangled fences, broken furniture and sodden remains of cardboard boxes, a smashed up bicycle, and loads of unrecognizable rubbish surrounded the sinister black bag.

The bag billowed in the middle. Water-filled, maybe. But no! A peak appeared in the bag, and if anyone had been close enough to inspect it, they would have seen the shapes of five fingertips, stretching the black nylon surface of the body bag, testingly. Then, with a sudden rip and a thrashing of water, the bag burst open and Jeff Abraham struggled out.

Except it was no longer Jeff Abraham. Still recognizable: yes. It had only been a matter of hours since his death, so decomposition had not claimed him, as it had certain of his zombie compatriots. Truth be

143

told, he had merely been bitten, not savaged or killed by a ghoul. Therefore he passed as human and living, although he was most certainly dead, and vampiric.

DECEMBER 25
5:37 A.M.

The Hummer sped wildly through the dark, muddy back road before coming to a screeching halt. The vehicle slid through the icy snow/mud mix at least twenty feet before stopping completely.

"We must get you to ground!" Henry announced as he turned from the driver's side seat to face Ralphie. "There is no way we are going to make it back to Talman's place before dawn."

"There's no need to rush, Henry." Ralphie said almost gleefully. "It's not like I'm going to burn up."

"What do you mean?" Talman asked quizzically. "You are a vampire! You will surely die with the first rays of dawn."

"We shall see now, won't we?" Ralphie replied.

Ralphie opened up the Hummer's left rear door and climbed out.

"What are you doing?" Henry called, now with obvious concern. He turned to his brother. "Has he lost his mind?"

Ralphie swiftly climbed a small hill near where the Hummer was parked. He moved with such a pace that it was difficult for the brothers to react, depart the vehicle, and catch up to him.

"Ah… there you are!" Ralphie announced to the bright orb coming up over the horizon. He giggled and began singing a verse from *The Age of Aquarius* "Let the sunshine in! Let the sunshine in!" and held out his arms – palms up – as if embracing it.

Smoke began to emit from the little boy's body and then, suddenly, nothing. Ralphie shook it off and smiled. "Well, gentlemen… satisfied?"

"What the fuck?" Henry grasped. "What sort of powers have you attained, Legion?"

"Ha, ha, ha," Ralphie laughed. "We are all about to find out."

He walked over to Talman and put his tiny hand on the bigger man's shoulder. "You, take me to the obelisk."

"But, I thought we were going back to my house," Talman protested.

"Not anymore. Plans have changed. And I think, for the better." He skipped back down the hill and stood by the black Hummer. "You, Talman, have helped me tonight more than you realize and if we don't go to the obelisk right away, you are both going to miss the fireworks!"

"Fireworks?" Henry mumbled to himself, sliding back down the slippery bank and joining Ralphie. "I can barely wait."

As the men got back into the vehicle, Talman added, "Since we are going to the obelisk, Henry, you best avoid going through Tarklin on your way to Melas. Drive the high road above Floyd Lake."

***

The Clarksburg Reporter
HUNDREDS DEAD – THOUSANDS MISSING
DISASTER HITS WEST VIRGINIA

Cities of Melas and Tarklin Completely Destroyed!
Floyd Lake bursts its barriers and sweeps everything
before it – Men, women and children devoured by
angry flood – Awful scenes witnessed by survivors.

CLARKSBURG, DECEMBER 25 – A cataclysmic
scene is reported from Tarklin. Early indications are
that this city of 15,000 inhabitants has been practically
wiped out of existence in the worst natural disaster in
West Virginia's history.

It is reported that Floyd Lake dam, five miles up
the valley above Melas, broke at around midnight last
night, struck by unseasonably high flood levels,
causing tremendous volumes of water to sweep down
the mountainside "like a tidal wave" to the West Fork
of the Monongahela River.

Witnesses claim it stood "over twenty feet in
height," gathering force as it tore along to Tarklin
seven miles below, sweeping everything before it.
Homes, schools, shopping centers and bridges were
overwhelmed in an instant, along with their human
occupants.

Water began over flowing the dam at about 7:30
p.m., when the West Virginia National Guard
announced flood warnings and voluntary evacuation
advice to Tarklin and residents down the valley. Hours
later the whole end of the dam gave way and the

contents of Floyd Lake swept everything before it: railroads, bridges and utility lines included.

The tidal wave first hit the neighboring town of Melas, reached a temporary plateau, drowning the deserted town. In its course onwards through a narrow bottleneck, its velocity and power increased.

Mr. Porter Sargent, 37, electrician, of Woodbridge Avenue, Tarklin said: "It was terrible. I warned my neighbors to leave, but they said they would put their trust in God. I just packed up the truck with my wife and kids and set off. By the time we were three miles down the road, the city was underwater. Only God knows if my neighbors survived."

Mrs. Jenna Sargent, 35, homemaker, reported, "The kids were watching out the back window all the time as we left. They said it was like a tsunami!"

Tyler Sargent, 15, student of Tarklin Road High School, said, "Looked like the whole place got swept away. Later on, me and my sister saw what looked like people up on the roofs of houses, but we didn't dare go back."

Mrs. Sargent added, "Goodness knows if we will ever be able to live in our lovely home again. It will take months, possibly years for us to get back to normal. Look at New Orleans."

The scene of the disaster has been entirely cut off from all communication since 2 o'clock this morning. Preliminary reports of the extent of the catastrophe were given by news helicopters above the valley. The city of Weston is on high alert...

CHAPTER 12

According to his GPS, it was an eighteen-hour drive from Tulsa, Oklahoma to Davis, West Virginia. Jay decided that he was going to make it today, no matter what, but as he approached the fifteenth hour in this "last leg" of the journey, he was beginning to reconsider the soundness of that decision.

Driving was atrocious. It got significantly worse ever since he crossed the West Virginia state line. And here he was, driving all night on Christmas Eve in terrible weather, four days into his road trip, and not far off his destination.

Still. Snow was good, wasn't it? At least it meant skiing was assured. He aimed to get to Davis on his birthday – tomorrow – and be skiing that afternoon, and his now-dirty Shelby Mustang had not let him down! He gripped the black leather steering wheel, still thrilled at his good fortune and still pleased with his purchase. Life was good.

Although he tried not to ponder on his nightmares and live in the moment instead, he couldn't help puzzling over the latest one, wondering why things had changed.

His latest dream last night was that a number of men were trapped in hellish chambers underground, either in tunnels in the earth, or in the deepest depths of hell – it was hard to distinguish – and attacked by horrific corpse-like creatures. He had helplessly observed them being killed in the most excruciatingly painful of ways. And the fear! There was a similar theme before – a gray world of defilement, and the pure painful fear of humans being pursued, tortured and killed by soulless beasts. But a different context, and a new character.

One of these beasts had travelled to the surface and begun transforming into a blood-sucking vampire-creature and was stalking various victims around a deserted town. This was a new permutation on the theme, but again, he felt powerless to stop the action. He could only watch, trying to distance himself from the hurt and protect himself from anguish, while chanting, "This is not real. This is a dream. I'll wake up in a minute."

Jay switched up the radio and sang along to the rock tunes.

Block it out. Block it all out.

It was now very early on Christmas morning. Still en route to Canaan Valley, Jay was traveling north on Interstate 79, south of Weston in weather that was frankly undrivable for his rear-wheel-drive Mustang.

"Dang it!" he cried, as his front end slewed on the ice of the road beneath his wheels. He swung his steering wheel around to compensate for the skid, and drove white-knuckled, peering through the sleety rain.

He approached the red taillights of a truck ahead, the end of a short roadblock. As they crawled along, he noticed road signs warning of a diversion and saw a sectioned-off area of roadway ahead.

This can't be good at all! he thought to himself as he stuck his head out the window, the sleet stinging his face.

A highway patrol police officer approached, his florescent jacket glaring through the weather.

"Sorry, Sir. There's been a flood. The West Virginia State Police have closed the Interstate due to flooding. We're directing you through Weston."

"Sorry to hear that, officer," Jay added.

"If I were you," the officer nodded at the beautiful Mustang, ill-equipped for the hazardous weather, "I'd hole up overnight till the weather improves. Stonewall Jackson Resort on the exit south of Weston is pretty close, and has good accommodations. We're due a good rainstorm which should clear it overnight."

"Thank you, officer," Jay raised his window, his dark curls already wet with frozen rain.

What a bummer! he mused. Despite his best intentions and determination to press on through the night, maybe that was madness. The detour would add miles, and the weather was crap. No other lunatics were on the road this late, in this weather. Except the police. Heck, yeah. Why not give himself a break? His back was tense, his hands aching with the tight claw-hold on the steering wheel.

He decided to get a room in that town or that Resort where the police were detouring traffic. It would soon be dawn, but he needed to rest.

He turned the wheel of the Mustang, reddening with anxiety when he felt the wheels turning uselessly on the icy road. The police officer pushed all his weight against the rear of the car, and the road wheels bit, and held.

"Thank you!" Jay cried, waving his arm out of the window, breathing a sigh of relief.

He kept driving through the rain, until it lessened, and the first light of dawn crept through the blackened skies.

He was traveling next to the river, which he could see was swollen way beyond its usual bank, since trees and bushes peeped from beneath the rushing waters. Wow! That was some flood. No wonder the bridge roads were shut off.

Then something caught his eye in the first light of dawn, moving with the current of water, but bigger than the other debris.

What? There were people, riding the current on something – a piece of house – a porch, maybe? Three people. A man, a woman, and a boy – a teen. A family floating downstream in floodwaters. They must need help.

It was far too cold and they must be drenched with frozen water. Jay feared the family might die of exposure or drown. What could he do? He drove alongside, with one eye on the river, one on the road, keeping pace with the flow of water, wondering how he could possibly stop them or help them.

"God help them!" he muttered. "Looks like they've saved themselves from disaster up to now. They deserve a helping hand!"

The river widened and the current slowed as the waters expanded widthwise. Jay saw that one of the guys was standing up and shunting the makeshift raft along sideways towards the bank of the river closest to the road. Good. Looked like it was shallower there, and although Jay couldn't see the edge of the river this side, because of the bank of the roadway and the drop of the river, he drove to the side and pulled the Mustang off the road to see what he could do.

The least he would be able to do was help the family up from the floodwaters. He parked up, opened the door to the cool air and set his boots into the icy slush. The rain had lightened in the growing daylight, but it was still very cold, and his breath hung in the air in white clouds with every exhalation.

He trudged as fast as he could through the slush of the rainy snow beside the road and clambered down the embankment to the level of the riverbank. His jeans were soaked through to his icy knees, but that was nothing compared to those poor people on the raft. Below him he could see them picking their way off the raft surface, and into the pebbled shallows, the boy and the man holding onto the edge of the wooden pallet, while the man extended one hand out to the woman, who was the last to get off.

By the time he scrambled down to them, they had each waded through the mud and stood on the riverbank, catching their breath – but only for a moment, because they looked ready to set off walking straight away. *What were they? Endurance athletes?*

"Hey!" called Jay, gently. He hadn't wanted to shout before, in case he put them off their stride and somebody lost their footing in the river.

All three looked at him in alarm, so he waved in a friendly manner and grinned. Maybe they'd thought he was about to say, "Get off my land!" so he was keen to indicate that he came in peace, and only to help them!

All three were white with shock and cold, soaked and disheveled.

"Here, let me help!" Jay held a hand out to help the woman up the embankment, "I have a car up there. Let me drive you somewhere – a hospital..." The woman shuddered and looked terrified, so he added, "... or wherever you want to go!"

"Thank you!" said the man, and gently supported the woman up the embankment. She held out her icy hand, and Jay took it in his. Now, close up, Jay could see that she didn't look old enough to be the mother of the teenage boy, unless looks were deceptive. Maybe the kid was her stepson? The man certainly was familiar towards her and acted proprietorial over her, having hugged her as soon as she hit dry land, and now steering her ass gently up the bank by holding her hips.

When the woman drew level, Jay held out his hand and hauled up the boy, and then the man. When all four were up the bank, Jay introduced himself.

"Johnnie, Amanda, and William," said the man, with a steady eye despite his shivering.

"Pleased to meet you," said Jay, "but let's get you into the warmth quickly! Get in!" he opened the Mustang's doors and reached in to unfold a tartan rag he'd kept on the backseat. He draped it around Amanda's shoulders.

"Oh, but your beautiful car!" protested Amanda, looking down at her soaked, mud-caked feet and legs.

"No worries," smiled Jay. "You're my priority. I've had the car a while, anyway!" he opened the trunk and rustled around in his suitcase before emerging with two towels and a heavy coat. He tossed them to Johnnie and William, saying, "Sorry, I'm not well-equipped but these might help a bit!"

When they were all settled into the car, Jay set the heater to full blast and set off tentatively back onto the road. Fortunately, or perhaps because of the extra weight in the car, the wheels held without spinning, and crunched over the ice, back onto the blacktop – wherever that was. Jay only had his old tire tracks to go by. No other traffic had gone by at all since he pulled off the road.

"Should I take you someplace to get checked out? Make sure you haven't got hyperthermia or something?"

"No," said Jonathan, not wishing to be in the company of any more doctors or nurses for a long time. "We'll be okay. We just need to get warm and dry."

"Where you headed?" asked Jay, and then laughed at himself. "I mean, I wasn't suggesting that this is normal, and you aimed to travel by raft to someplace specific.

"What I mean is – I'm going to the Stonewall Jackson Resort now. How about I see if I can get us all rooms? My treat. It's my birthday, after all. I'll put you up for the night, get you fed, your clothes can dry properly, and we can all spend some time recuperating while we wait out the storm?"

"Happy birthday!" Amanda said gratefully, her teeth still chattering while her body adjusted to the rapid change in temperature.

Jonathan, sitting in the front passenger seat, his mind still frozen in survival mode, turned around to judge Amanda and Willie's reactions. They both looked drawn and exhausted. After all they'd gone through in the last twenty-four hours, this guy and his talk of normal life was a godsend.

"Sounds great. We can't thank you enough," said Jonathan. "But I don't know how we can repay you. If you give us your contact details…"

"Nah!" Jay waved one hand dismissively, still watching the road. "I've had some good luck, good business deals. I like to spread the good fortune a little. Let me feel like I'm helping, please!"

Ah, well, Jonathan thought. A guy driving a car like this, who could afford a brand new Ford Shelby Mustang GT500 with all the top of the range gadgets and customizations and yet treat it like a pick-up truck – filling it with muddy, soaked strangers, must be a millionaire or something. He could afford it, he guessed. Hell, after what they'd been through, they could do with some kindness and pampering.

"I still want to pay you back," Jonathan asserted.

"Don't give it a second's thought. Your good company is reward enough. It can get lonely driving, so I'm glad to make your acquaintance. I just wish it hadn't been under these circumstances. I'd much rather have met you in a diner, got chatting and offered you a lift!"

"God moves in mysterious ways," William piped up from the back.

Funny thing to say... thought Jay *...especially from a boy.*

William thought the same thing. He didn't know why he'd said that either. It was as if he'd said it without thinking, or as if someone else was speaking through him. He might be a priest, but he didn't expect to be speaking in tongues, yet he just opened his mouth and those words came out. He puzzled over it himself.

Jay settled into driving through the rain, which had recommenced heavily. He demisted the windshield, realizing that he was delighted by the steam coming from his new travel companions as they warmed up. That meant they were drying out, getting back to normal body temperature. *Where there's heat there's life* came into his head.

"Yes, God moves in a mysterious way!" repeated Jay, feeling suddenly joyous. "His wonders to perform."

Then he spent the next five minutes wondering where that quote had come from. *And why a good Jewish boy was quoting from some* goyim *hymnal.* He mused. *What a* meshuggener!

"How did you guys end up on the river anyway?" Jay asked, after a few moments. No one answered, as if they were thinking about what to say.

Then Johnnie struck up, "Walking home from a party..."

"One hell of a party!" exclaimed Amanda, talking through the rug she clutched tight over her nose. "Damn! I think I broke a nail!"

"We slipped off the bridge, clambered onto those boards," added the boy, William.

Jay whistled, "You're lucky to be alive!"

"We sure are," Jonathan muttered grimly, through gritted teeth.

They drove in silence for a while, all three of the rescued glad for the chance to rest in the warmth of Jay's heater, and try to work through some of the events in their own minds.

Jay – for all that he liked company – knew they must be in shock and was sensitive to their need to recover. Little did he know quite how shocking the last twenty-four hours had been for them!

After a while, Jay asked, "Anyone know where this Stonewall Resort is?"

"Not far. Along this road. Exit 91 to Roanoke." Jonathan said, pointing a heavy forefinger and suddenly realizing how exhausted he was. "There's a right turn on US-19 South. It's about two or three miles from the interstate. Just follow the signs to Stonewall Resort State Park. The entrance... on your left."

"You sound as tired as me, and I've been driving for seventeen hours, from Tulsa."

"Only... Twenty four hou-urs from Tulsa!" Amanda sang, sleepily in a very bad Gene Pitney impression.

"Not quite," smiled Jay from the rear view mirror. "Although it might as well be."

William was still shivering, white-faced, and Amanda snuggled against his shoulder, trying to share her body warmth.

"You sure you don't need some medical help, you guys?" Jay's concerned voice rose above the soft hum of the heater and the sound of the driving sleet outside.

"No! No. Just... rest, I reckon," Jonathan turned a blank expression towards Jay.

Jay shook his head, sucking his teeth in an expression of doubt. He wanted to help these people, but they were determined not to let him take them to a doctor. *Some people, you just couldn't understand,* he supposed.

"Thanks anyway. You're already our knight in shining armor," muttered Amanda.

"Riding my white Mustang," added Jay, smiling.

He drove on further, until Jonathan stirred into action.

"Here's the turn-off on the road," Jonathan sat up, "Nearly there."

Jay indicated and swung right, and they travelled on.

"Not sure I'd be able to ski in this weather today anyway, so – no loss that I'm not at my planned destination. This will be fine for all of us.

"Hopefully, after we get some rest, the weather might have cleared." Jay said, more to himself than anyone else. His newfound friends hadn't been too chatty up to now, but hey – they were probably as exhausted as he was.

The huge main Lodge building overlooked the icy gray expanse of Stonewall Jackson Lake, but looked beautiful.

He parked the Mustang, and they all entered the spacious foyer, still wrapped in their motley collection of plaid rugs, blankets, and coats.

"Wow! This is crazy nice," said William, rubbing his eyes.

"Welcome to Stonewall Resort!" smiled the chirpy check-in clerk at the desk. "Merry Christmas to you all! May I ask if you folks have a booking today, please?"

Jay looked shocked. This place looked massive – what if there were no rooms? It was the early hours of Christmas Day. The girl saw the look on his face and added quickly, "We have plenty of room, sir! Would you like Lodge rooms or a Cottage, please?"

Jay opted for rooms in the main Lodge. He had no intention of tramping out into the cold again after all this time. He turned to his three companions.

"Um. How many rooms do you need?" He didn't like to make assumptions about Jonathan and Amanda sleeping together.

"We'll share a family room," said Jonathan, "You've been very generous as it is."

Jay laughed, "No problem. My treat."

While Jay filled in his details as they checked in, the clerk took a good look at the dirty and ragged, wrinkled and still-wet state of Jay's friends. She tried not to show distaste at this set of ragamuffins checking into the establishment, but she was concerned.

"Gosh – are you okay? You look like you're half-drowned!"

"The floods…" began Jonathan.

159

"Oh my goodness, yes – I've just been watching the news on TV! The storm – it's terrible. You know, there are bridges down and roads flooded!"

"Yeah, we know." Amanda muttered.

"It's dreadful, isn't it? First snow, then rain, then floods. Practically like the seven plagues of Egypt!" the clerk rattled on, "I mean, there are probably people dead out there!"

"Hmm," said Jay, pushing over the check-in form and taking two key cards from the girl's outstretched hand.

"Thank you, sir. Is there anything else you'd like to enhance your stay? Chocolate dipped strawberries? Champagne breakfast? Spa facilities and massage?"

Four pairs of weary eyes gazed at her blankly.

"Clothes," said Jay. "These folks lost their luggage. Do you have any clothes for sale?"

"Well, we have a gift shop, but I'm afraid it doesn't open on Christmas Day."

All four of them stared at the clerk, impassively. She got the message.

"But of course, under the circumstances, I will get someone to open it up for you now, sir," she added quickly, picking up the telephone receiver and punching in a number.

"Why don't you go on up, take warm showers and I'll fetch you some fresh clothes and provisions," Jay passed over one of the key cards to Jonathan, "I'll bring them up as soon as I can."

"Choose me something stylish, just like me," Amanda opened her plaid rug to reveal her filthy jacket and blouse, grinning under her stringy, half-frizzed hair.

"I'll see what I can do," Jay nodded, as the other three made their way to their room.

"Hey, can we get some food sent up?" Jay asked the clerk.

"Well, breakfast is served in our restaurant in an hour... Or certainly, there is our in-room dining menu." She passed him a menu, which he scanned in seconds.

"Yes. Everything, please," he said. "Sent up to their room and I'll join them."

"Everything?"

"Yes. All that's on here. The granola, the French toast, the pancakes, the waffle; the eggs every which way; the omelet. The biscuit and sausage gravy, bacon, ham, more sausage, grits... and all the drinks. For four people. Please."

"Yes, of course sir." She scribbled frantically.

Then Jay followed a male member of the hotel staff who had promptly appeared with the key to open up the gift shop.

***

Jonathan let them into the large, airy room.

"Wow!" said William, delighted to see a luxurious haven after their recent exploits. "Can we just sleep straight off, now?"

"Shower first, young man!" said Amanda, "You have to let me auntie you a little. Besides, you're filthy and these beds are pristine!"

"Like we haven't got wet enough tonight!" grumbled William, still a young teenage boy for all his maturity and priesthood. He wandered into the bathroom and the sound of the shower spray soon signaled his intention to obey her instructions.

Amanda and Jonathan sank into the chairs, exhausted.

"Are we safe here?" asked Amanda.

Jonathan nodded, "Safe as anywhere. Safer than most."

"Shit." Amanda rubbed her face, smearing muddy marks around her cheeks. "What the hell exactly went on there with those fucking corpses and blue flashes and shit?"

Jonathan shrugged his shoulders, too tired to discuss his suspicions now.

By the time Jay came upstairs and knocked on the door, armed with carrier bags of clothing, snacks and drinks, William and Amanda were snug in fluffy white bath robes, and Jonathan was just toweling off in the bathroom. None of them had luxuriated in the shower, all of them simply wanting to be clean and warm and asleep as soon as possible.

Just behind Jay, staff pushing two trolleys of hot breakfast food, juices, teas and coffees arrived.

"Oh, wow!" William said, falling upon the food as soon as the waiters had removed the lids of the dishes.

"God, you're good!" Amanda smiled at Jay, grabbing poached eggs and toast, smashing them with her fork and scooping up hot yellow yolk on toast into her mouth as fast as she could.

None of them could recall the last time they'd eaten.

"Funny, I didn't even realize I was hungry till now!" Jonathan said, devouring maple pancakes, "And now I realize I'm famished!"

Jay sat on one of the beds, sawing with his knife at a plate of ham, eggs and bacon on his knee. Okay, so he hadn't eaten kosher for years. Not a very good Jewish boy at all. *So sue me!* He just had a need for red meat. Protein.

"I say we all eat ourselves unconscious, get some rest for a few hours, and you meet me for lunch later in Stillwaters Restaurant – downstairs, about 1 p.m.?"

"Sounds good to us!" Jonathan answered for all of them.

To their surprise, considering the overwhelming amount of food, they ate almost everything that was delivered. Even the granola. And the fruit salad.

William was already finding it hard to keep his eyes open. His carbohydrate overload had suddenly shut down his system and he longed for sleep.

"I'll bid you a good night, despite it being 6:30 in the morning!" Jay got up to go to his room next door satisfied in body and soul – and exhausted to the point of hysteria.

***

Seventeen hours from yesterday's starting point in Tulsa, the recent hours of driving in awful weather with full concentration and tension of all muscles, followed by rescuing near-drowning strangers – and

163

sorting out their needs – had taken it out of him. As soon as Jay's head hit the proverbial pillow, he found himself in a sound sleep; straight into REM and the dreaming stage.

Jay found himself in his dream, watching a man becoming a vampire. Then he remembered his previous night's dream. It was picking right up where it left off! Worse still, Jay felt himself becoming present in the scene, and the action seemed to be happening in the present, right now! Whatever he saw, and felt, was happening now:

Jay feels uncomfortable. He's never felt this way before. He's trained himself to be detached, impassive, and an observer. Although he knows this is still a dream, it's feeling more real, in real time. Although Jay is here in the dream, the characters still can't see him. No one notices or interacts with him. In fact, there's no one else here but Jay and the vampire man.

The vampire man is wandering, confused, through the desolate town. Jay has no empathy with this creature, but senses that the vampire is dying of hunger and is unstoppably driven by a need for blood. He is literally bloodthirsty.

Staggering around, the vampire searches unsuccessfully for some sign of humanity, flinging open the doors of stores and houses, but the place is a ghost town. Worse, it's as if everyone has up and left; just abandoned the place in a matter of hours, rather than the slow years of decline of most towns that fall into ruin gradually through the lack of industry or work.

This town has recently been inhabited, but stores are left stocked but unstaffed, cars abandoned in the street. Houses have dinner laid on the table, long grown cold. But there's no one to be seen. It's as if the town remains as if lived in, ready for crowds of people to continue their lives. Yet there is no sign of life. Just a tattered man, unliving and yet undead, desperate for what he needs, his nerves and muscles crying for relief, crying for his fix – like a junkie.

The vampire's nose twitches, alive to the scent of blood. He turns his head sharply towards Jay, all senses on the alert.

Jay holds his breath: for an awful moment fearing that this particular dream – this different dream – might mean that he could fall victim to this beast. Because it is a different feeling in this dream – it is all too real; all too present; all too "now." Jay's blood runs cold in his veins, and he is afraid to breathe for fear that he gives himself away.

But the vampire moves on. Stalking through the streets, searching for prey. And although Jay has no sense that he is following him on foot, he is with him all the time, at his shoulder. There is no escape.

Ahead, in the darkness, there's something white. It's night-time, Jay realizes. Of course it is! It has been all along! *This is when I sleep, of course!* he rationalizes. *It's because I'm dreaming at night! And that's when the horrors come. The vampires and the ghouls. It's night.*

Part of Jay's conscious awareness suddenly kicked in: *I fell asleep in daytime. We've just had breakfast.*

But it's night. And the vampire's step is quickening as he hurries towards the large white van in the middle of the street. And Jay is still with him, hurrying at the same pace, although he's not aware that he's walking. Jay's not even aware that he has legs. He looks down, and sees that he has – and they're bizarrely wearing golfing trousers, but he is gliding along, not having to walk at all.

Drawing away his gaze back to the vampire, he sees him ripping off the back door of the van. Jay can see the Red Cross on the side of the white van. Inside, the fridges, the hooks, the shelves, chairs, and table show Jay that it's a mobile blood donation service: a bloodmobile! The one creature most in desperate need of blood has hit pay dirt. The vampire grabs plastic bags of blood, bites off the stoppers and starts sucking at them like slurpies.

Jay can smell the metallic tang of blood. *Dang it! I can even taste the coppery iron on my tongue,* his mind raced. *I don't like this dream!*

He repeated his affirmation to glean some comfort from the nightmare. *And it is a dream. Just a dream. It isn't real!* Despite the affirmation, he still was riveted to the scene before him…

The man – the vampire – is sucking the packages of blood dry, squeezing out every drop with his long, taloned fingers; then tossing them aside, and picking up the next. He sucks hungrily, like a child at the teat of a bottle, his eyes popping greedily.

He belches a bloody bubble from his lips that bursts, spattering blood down his chin. He grins grotesquely, with bloodstained teeth, delighted by his fortuitous find. But there's not enough blood.

There's never enough blood! Jay senses. And now he's frightened, because he doesn't want to feel what this beast feels. He doesn't want to know.

But it's as if this vampire man doesn't know quite what to do with this new life. Or death. He is simply driven by his need for blood, but can find it nowhere, until now. But then, it's not really fresh blood, is it? Not warm, fresh blood, straight from the vein, spurting softly into his mouth. He can imagine that. And that's what he wants. Living, breathing blood, alive with oxygen and energy. Human blood from a living being.

That's what I crave! Jay jumps in alarm. It's not him. No. NO.

I don't like this! Get me out of this dream! It's a dream! It's not real!

But the vampire is awake, and aware of his new purpose he lurks in darkened corners, ambling around the empty streets and empty buildings, wandering in the debris of a wrecked and deserted town, looking for blood. The fresher the better.

And then his nose is twitching again. Jay can feel it – the urge, the drive, the smell of blood. And this time it isn't cold blood from plastic bags in a fridge. It's a pulsating, throbbing hum of blood passing through veins and venules to the heart, arteries and arterioles away from the heart to other organs. The tiniest capillaries seem to be calling out a siren song, luring him.

Luring who? Jay asked, desperately. *The vampire! It's the vampire! Not me.*

But still he senses the vampire's longing, understands his craven desire. He feels the desperate need within the creature's inhuman heart. He hears the distant rush of blood; the opening of valves as fresh, warm, blood pumps through a living body.

And with the vampire – in body, mind and spirit – unwillingly, Jay is swept away through the streets of that dark, gray, ramshackle ghost town, in search of the nearest living human who can satisfy the craving. Momentarily at least.

Jay's mouth is dry. He wants to shout; to cry out the words that will break this terrible spell: *This isn't real! It's just a dream! It's not real! I can wake up! I just need to wake!*

"Are you awake?"

The hammering on the door was now accompanied by words.

"Jay! Are you awake?"

Jay flicked open his eyes. His heart was still beating fast, thundering in his chest. He sat up, wondering where the hell he was. Nowhere he recognized, but light was flooding through the curtains.

"Jay? It's William!" said the voice behind the bedroom door.

"Urrgh!" groaned Jay, and flew out of bed in his boxers, unlocking the door and trying to open his eyes wide and alert.

"Sorry, Jay," William shrugged, "were you still asleep?"

"What? Who? Me? No! Course not! Ha!" Jay said rapidly, clearly overcompensating for an unconvincing appearance.

"It's just, it's 12:55, so we thought we'd go down to lunch together. Like you said. But if you need some more time…" William glanced down at Jay's boxers.

"No. No. I'm ready!" grinned Jay, scratching his beard and winking against the light.

"Uh-huh. So I see. You wanna give us a knock next door when you're set to go?" William backed off.

"One minute!" said Jay, "I'll just pull on some clothes."

"Well, I hope you got yourself the same uniform!" came Amanda's voice. She appeared in the doorway dressed in the same outfit as William: beige golf trousers and a blue sweatshirt reading: STONEWALL RESORT, STILLWATER.

"Stylish, my ass!" she declared, and turned on her heel.

CHAPTER 13

From a distance, they saw the misty aura of the green, throbbing glow before they saw the ten-foot-tall stone obelisk itself. It was humming with a low-pitch sound and glowing with an eerie, shifting, green light by the time Dr. Henry Cane and his brother Talman arrived, along with the small but intimidating figure of Ralphie. As they all rushed forward in anticipation, the two brothers came suddenly to a dead halt and stood there in shock and fury.

"No!" cried Henry, grimacing in pain.

Before their eyes, a cloud of wispy, ethereal forms that mingled in the air like ribbons of cigarette smoke whirled into one funnel and shot towards the obelisk itself. Hundreds of obscure, translucent humanoid figures transfigured into smoke, were being sucked like a vacuum into the mass of the granite-like structure. Like the eye of a storm, the stone obelisk was the still center, attracting a series of concentric swirls of matter, and it stood immobile, absorbing it all within itself.

"Shit," grimaced Talman. "Is that what I think it is?"

Ralphie, his chubby child's jaw set with determination, trod onwards. A steely glint played in his eyes as he approached the site of the obelisk, throbbing green, continually sucking hundreds of damned souls into its vortex.

Talman had ensured that this obelisk was safely transported to his colleague and earthly master, Victor Rothenstein, back in the 1930s. It looked innocently like a blank stone memorial column, the kind that might be seen marking the grave of an auspicious citizen – until it was activated.

It came from Transylvania, the land of Vlad Dracula – Vlad the Impaler – and the homeland of the blood-drinking, blood-bathing Countess Erzsébet Báthory – who cruelly tortured, bled and killed 650 young women. From such a site of intense evil and serial killing, it was imbued not only with the pure – or should that be "impure" – essence of human wickedness, but also with incredible powers to unleash Hell on earth. It represented an effective electrical conductor for evil forces, and when combined with the earthbound powers of evildoers, necromancers, vampires, ghouls, and demons on earth, its effects could be cataclysmic.

Up to now, Ralphie had regularly visited the obelisk in the dead of night to commune with the demonic forces, to absorb the strength of Legion, and to enrich his own evil powers and knowledge, until he had an all-encompassing knowing and connection. This was called the "collective consciousness" that enabled Ralphie to control the undead ghouls and have them do his will as one.

Except it wasn't Ralphie's will; it was the demon Legion's. But in order to get to this point, Ralphie had sat for many hours, hypnotized and entranced by the sinister luminescent pulsation of the rock, and the tiny imperceptible hum that assailed his ears.

During earlier communes with the demon, Ralphie had felt the increasing force of Legion surge within him. That had filled his tiny mind with visions of disaster, which he grew to learn were preludes to the End Times. Already, Ralphie had used these powers to activate the undead across the nearby towns.

He had vividly seen the image of ghouls reanimating through the force of his thoughts: staggering to their feet, wailing and moaning. Driven by an unimaginable hunger, they voraciously sought humans to eat, thirsting for blood, and eager to devour the flesh of mortals.

Now, Ralphie was so, so much stronger, and the indistinguishable hum of the obelisk too was increasing, like a machine whirring to a greater crescendo. Ralphie had come a long way since he was an innocent and newly dead – and undead – boy. There was nothing of his childish humanity or frailty remaining. Since then, he and the demon Legion had become one. But no one knew that the Legion self that had previously taken over Ralphie had flown off to conduct its evil elsewhere, driven by Lucifer himself to vacate Ralphie's body.

And greater still – unbeknownst to Henry and Talman – Ralphie was now at one with Lucifer himself. Satan was amongst them. The father had returned to Earth, incarnate, to complete what his sons had started.

Henry and Talman were oblivious to this fact.

Many had tried to destroy the obelisk, including Jonathan and William, under instruction from the late, great vampire hunter and William's priest-mentor, Father Alex Van Helsing. But none had succeeded. From its sledgehammered and crumbled remains, the obelisk had always reconstituted itself. None had thought to separate and remove the pieces from the site to ensure that they could never reassemble back into this characterless channel of evil – this stony pillar of the damned.

Even so, the obelisk alone would not be sufficient of itself to unleash Hell's dreadful hordes. It needed the combination of human and Satanic power to energize it, and it had fed from Ralphie's absorption of Legion as much as Ralphie and Legion had fed from it. Now that Satan walked the earth the potency of it was unimaginable.

Victor and others had worked tirelessly for years to install the obelisk here, in the vicinity of the old Madison house, and then to open the gateway to Hell that it represented, and that it would facilitate when the time was right. Talman and Henry had battled for centuries to reach this point, assuming many bodily forms and many roles to fulfill their morbid destiny. Henry had never felt it to be so close since the 1940s, and his glory days in the Nazi SS, embodied as he was as Heinrich Himmler. What a shame it was, Henry thought, that they had been defeated – albeit momentarily – in their wicked intent. It had been very close at hand. So close, Henry could almost taste it. How close they had all been, then, to opening up the gates of Hell!

That time was coming… and this time, they would succeed. But for now – here was the obelisk, drinking in the souls of the dead and the doomed, instead of driving out the souls already trapped in Hell! All of them knew that the process must be reversed, and the portal must be opened, like a gaping, toothless and diseased mouth, to vomit up the damned from the bowels of the Underworld.

The obelisk's strange green light changed in tone and shade, pulsating alternately from bright green to dark green. The thrumming sound it made was like a heartbeat – in the heart of darkness.

Ralphie approached the base of the structure, grimly frowning, and stared hard at the pulsing light. His whole body began to pulsate too, in rhythm with the regular fluctuations of the green illumination. He sensed the power of Hell surging within him, rejuvenating the vestiges of the demonic strength he had drawn from Legion, and the new Satanic presence that had been growing inside his tiny, undead child's body over recent days.

Ralphie raised his arms and extended his chubby fingers, like starfish. In any other child it would have indicated a desire to be lifted up by his dad. But this was no longer a child, and the father he extolled was the Satanic force within him. No, he was seeking only to harness the energy to his own deadly ends.

Henry and Talman took up position behind Ralphie, creating a triangular, arrow-like formation, with Ralphie as the sharp point, directly in front of the obelisk. His face mirrored the changing greenness, the reflected light casting a ghoulish tinge over his pale, freckled expression, as if he was watching a flickering old movie. The physical body of Ralphie acknowledged profound sensations within it. The green glow of the obelisk grew to a vividly blinding green and the throbbing, pulsating rhythm consumed Ralphie's body, thundering like a heartbeat, as if he was alive again.

Ralphie felt that familiar, overwhelming power rising up inside him, filling his tiny body, thrilled with the supreme knowing he had gleaned from Legion, Lucifer lighting a fire ablaze within.

And all the time, the steadily increasing hum assailed their ears, filling their minds, and the souls of the dead whipped into the surface of the obelisk, like the silvery tails of salmon rushing to spawn.

Meanwhile, the spawn of the devil stood either side of the demonic devil child, and knew what had to be done. They needed to perform a ritual to bring back some of the tormented souls from Hell and have them reinhabit their bodies here on earth. The legions of the damned would soon assemble and the forces of evil would increase in preparation for Satan's apocalyptic final solution.

Henry, Talman, and Lucifer in the form of Ralphie, all kept their hands raised. Lucifer/Ralphie began to chant in a strange archaic language to begin the secret ritual of necromancy. After the initial exhortation by Lucifer/Ralphie in ancient Aramaic, the whirling souls flashing by their heads diminished and then vanished, but the green pulsating aura of the obelisk intensified, and the loud humming sound, having worked its way up to a drone, became louder still.

Henry and Talman Cane also began to intone the same demonic incantations, forming an eerie, echoing chorus. All three voices chanting together were suddenly joined by the booming voice of Legion, who had landed behind them to take up his part of the ritual. The brothers were so focused on the obelisk that they were unaware of the white-winged bat behind them and assumed the voice was Lucifer/Ralphie's.

Now the words spoken in unison appeared to make the ground shake with its force: "We commune together to complete the Great Plan! To progress the End Times!"

A great groan emanated from deep within the obelisk and the ground shook. Henry and Talman cast looks at each another, gleams of excitement and satisfaction in their eyes.

"We call upon the souls of the damned to rise!" Legion's voice roared.

A distant sound of wailing and moaning seemed to emanate from beneath the earth itself.

Then the unbearably loud voice of Legion intoned again: "It is time to ARISE!"

The deep, rich booming voice of Legion filled the air with an almost tangible force, shuddering the earth and making the obelisk before them rattle with deep vibrations, its green pulse throbbing faster and faster. Suddenly, there was a blinding light, then an earth-shattering rumble, followed by a thunderous creak.

The very Earth's crust began to crack, the soil beneath blistering up through the grass. Great fissures split the ground under the obelisk a short distance from where they stood, unsettling their positions.

With a massive roar that signaled a great upheaval in the ground beneath their feet, their necromancy took effect and the souls of the dead they had called upon began to return to earth.

From the depths of the cracked, black earth, unearthly screams broke forth; followed by the most hideous stench of putrid, decaying flesh, and the slow, painful "birth" of grotesque, misshapen, shadowy figures pushing their way out from within the broken soil.

The extreme ugliness of these souls in transit was indescribable. Talman gave a small involuntary cry. Even Henry – who had witnessed much to appall the hardest man these past four hundred years – was startled by the sight of so many sickening, putrefying faces; like melted wax, bloated and unrecognizable as human. Of course, they were not human.

But the gross ugliness of the physical form of these tormented creatures was a metaphor for the true, appalling evil of their souls, and the horrible deeds that had consigned them to Hell in the first place.

Two dozen or more horrifying, opaque but filmy forms came pouring out of the base of the obelisk. The stone monument was still throbbing with light, but its droning hum was now drowned out by the ear-splitting shrieks and wails of the tormented souls as they were released into the world once again.

They spewed out of the bowels of the earth, then floated up and hung in the air like ragged, dirty laundry, forming a nauseatingly horrific curtain of death – a signal for Hell on earth.

177

They wavered as if uncertain, wailing with their deformed mouths and molten features twisting in paroxysms of hatred and fury. The sight, sound and the stench of them were fit to curdle milk. No living man or woman had witnessed such malformed and freakish grossness. It was the unimaginable; worse than the sickest mind could imagine. A nightmare incarnate, all the more terrifying because this was real.

Talman, sweating, turned aside and vomited, bent over with his hands on his knees. He coughed up a mixture of dry heaves and bile – which smelled sweeter than the air around him – then shakily stood upright again. Wiping his sour-tasting lips, he gave an apologetic glance to Henry, who scowled back at him in fury.

Ralphie stared fixedly at the wall of shrouds before him unaffected by the sickening sight, since he was no longer a boy, with a child's sensibilities. He was almost entirely demon, merely inhabiting the body of a child. And the part of him that wasn't demon, was Lucifer himself.

So foul was the sight, that when Ralphie gave a flourish of his hands and the ghostly forms flew off in their separate directions, Talman laughed aloud in relief. The putrid smell of them still hung in the air, and the horrifying images of them were still burned into Talman's retinas, but he knew that they had gone – at least from that place, collectively.

The souls who had once been sucked into Hell where they were trapped and tortured were now returned to earth. They had flown out to seek their dead earthly bodies.

Within minutes, they would be reunited with their bodily remains, and the dead would soon rise as zombies, under Ralphie's command. With a single thought, he could control them as one.

Ralphie tossed back his head and laughed a deep, demonic laugh. Simultaneously, the obelisk glowed stronger and the droning sound became loud enough to burst an eardrum. The rumbling that had started beneath the obelisk and cracked the earth around it began again, this time truly shaking the ground for miles around.

Henry and Talman braced their feet against the earth, but both were knocked down by the thundering of an earthquake. They sprawled on the ground, sinking their fingers into the dewy grass to find purchase to clamber back on their feet again.

Talman chose to remain on his knees, hoping and waiting for the shaking of the earth to stop. When he looked up, he saw Ralphie, backlit by the blinding green light of the obelisk behind him. He remained on his feet, his arms stretched skywards, laughing manically. He was drinking in the increasing power of the obelisk and relishing it.

Tectonic plates shifted as the earth unrolled miles beneath the surface with a sinister grumble. If the full power of the earthquake was merely restricted to the area immediately surrounding the obelisk, the rippling effect of it reached farther.

The undulating waves of Earth's unrest shook the very foundations of the cemetery two miles away. First the ground trembled and the trees surrounding the graveyard vibrated. Then a deep groaning sound signaled the cracking of the dirt paths and the rumpling of the manicured lawn, the spewing out of rich dark soil, and the shifting of gravestones as the ground beneath them rolled. Some grave markers toppled to the ground, while others dropped askew. But from certain of the graves themselves, came the worst.

Meantime, through the fetid air, the howling, ragged membranous souls of the damned flew from the obelisk – the gateway to Hell – to a number of the graves, and shot straight into the earth where the buried lay. All was silent.

There was a scrabbling, and a loosening of the shifted soil, an uprooting, like the creation of a molehill. From the shifting mounds, fingers clawed their way out from the grave, dirt spraying from the rapid activity of the gray soily fingers. Then a whole hand emerged, grabbing, seeking some purchase and finding a clump of solid ground. Or a grotesque, half decomposed head. Arms shot out of the grave and began to dig the earth around them, and then the dirt-covered face of a corpse would be uncovered. Heads and shoulders emerged, and strong arms braced themselves on either side of the grave to heave themselves up, like a person rising out of a bath. Others crawled head first, dressed in their funeral shrouds or best clothes.

The dead were walking the Earth again. But only a few. Only twenty or so: those specific corpses from the areas around Tarklin. The damned. The lost. Those who had performed acts of evil or sin on earth, and were paying for them in Hell.

Back at the obelisk, the ritual was completed as far as it could be. Henry was bewildered. He had counted only twenty-four souls pouring forth from the base of the obelisk, although admittedly, he had been thrown from his feet and didn't see all that might have happened. But certainly, this was nothing like the outpouring of all Hell's damned souls he had anticipated. The obelisk itself stood dimly stony, as if all its energy had been expended in opening the gates of Hell for just that apocalyptic moment. Ralphie grinned in satisfaction, his arms folded, and his feet spread firmly on the land. Henry had found his feet again on the churned-up soil long before, whereas Talman had been kneeling in a fetal position, his arms clasped over his head. He slowly unwrapped himself, conscious now that the earth had stopped moving, the screams and droning had abated, and all was still and relatively quiet.

Until, in a flash, the great thundering roar of displaced air and the thrashing of leathery wings signaled the arrival of Legion, in the recognizable form of a huge white bat. The obelisk began to gear up again, its throbbing hum and rhythmical illumination building up energy, the green glow spreading again. With a final, braking flap of his wings, the demon landed and came to a halt next to Ralphie.

Henry and Talman gaped at the sight of them both standing together, and separate. Legion should be inside Ralphie. He was inside him.

Wasn't he?

Confusion struggled across their faces, as they tried to make sense of what they were seeing – and what it meant. What had happened?

"But... But... Ralphie's here!" stammered Talman, aghast. "How can he metamorphose into Legion – and still be here?"

Henry said nothing, his jaws clenching in anger. He hated it when he didn't understand something. His cold, analytical mind liked to rationalize things, and this made no sense at all to him. It wasn't logical, even within the constraints of illogical demonic magic and other Dark Arts. It just didn't compute.

Ralphie laughed his demonical laugh again, and bellowed again in Legion's voice, "Hahaha! Your faces! This was worth it to see the expressions on your worthless faces! Hahahaha!"

The huge white bat shuffled its clawed feet in frustration, and it screeched in the same Legion voice, "Fools! Fools! I am Legion!"

"No! I am Legion!" bawled Ralphie, then laughed, bending forward, holding his sides as if they might split. "Hahaha! This just... gets better! Hahaha!"

"Who are you?" chorused the bat, Henry, and Talman, addressing Ralphie, who wiped tears from his eyes, and tried to swallow down the laughter which kept rising within him, scrabbling out like the dead arising from their graves.

Henry glowered, fixing Ralphie with a malevolent stare.

"Now, now my son..." the voice had changed to a soothing tone. Still authoritative, but with a manipulative edge. Its effects upon Henry and Talman

182

were immediate and shocking. Their mouths dropped in fear, their eyes boggling wide in disbelief.

"Hahaha!" Ralphie laughed, a nasty tone in the chuckles this time. "So you know me now, my boys?"

"F...father?" began Talman.

"Father, Lucifer, Satan, Baal, Beelzebub, Mammon, Antichrist, Chief of the Demons, Prince of Darkness, Evil One, Iblis, Kroni, Shaitan, Mephistopheles, Voland, Kolski, Belial, Old Nick, Angra Mainyu, Dark Lord, Diabolos, Der Leibhaftige, Azazel!" roared Ralphie. "All of these and so much more! We are all so much more than the label others give us! Hahaha!"

The satanic laughter echoed around the area, blasting the brothers' eardrums.

"I thought I'd better keep an eye on you," Satan's voice boomed, threateningly now, "because you have been known to FAIL!" The final word reverberated in the brothers' ear canals, rattling their brains.

They stood, shamefaced, taking in their father's words, until Legion gave a low, dissatisfied growl. He stamped his feet in irritation.

"Well! Get me out of this," complained Legion, extending his white batwings, like the great sheets of sailboats. "I can't get out. I'm stuck as a fucking bat!"

"Legion, I have more pressing engagements. As we all have," Satan said in a mocking tone. "Look at me! Hardly a fitting vestment for the Antichrist!" He looked down at Ralphie's child body. Then he pulled the waistband of his pants and peered down within, adding lewdly, "But highly amusing, nonetheless!"

Legion gave a rumble of dissent, scraping his claws against the hillocks of dirt, like a bull preparing to charge.

"I will not tolerate insubordination!" warned Ralphie's steely glare. Legion stood still, his gray-white fluffy bat-head, leathery pointed ears and beady eyes lowered in submission.

Ralphie continued. "Now we are, all four, assembled; with our collective knowledge, will and energies, we can now invoke the full power of darkness and unleash the entire forces of Hell!"

Talman's stomach churned, and the bitter taste of bile washed over his tongue. The foretaste he'd had of the horrors to come had been bad enough. Dammit, maybe he had too much human blood running through his veins. Even though their mother was a witch, she had "communed" in a physical sense with Satan himself. Maybe he was more his mother's son, as much as he hated to admit it. He had never been as tolerant and impassive to evil as his brother Henry with his cold, calculating malevolence. But this was no time to wimp out now. It had taken them both over four hundred years to get to this point – and for their father it had been millennia. No, he should be very proud of his heritage, and the part he was playing in The End Times. So he swallowed down the rising bile and nausea, gave his head a shake, focused on his father's words, and concentrated on the matter in hand.

The four took up position in front of the obelisk and raised their arms. Except for Legion, who held himself back slightly behind the other three figures in human form, scowling. He lifted his long, elegant, hollow-boned and aerodynamic wing structure to create an impermeable white barrier against prying eyes and the prevailing wind. He also formed the shaft point to their arrowhead formation, and strengthened the very whole.

"Now we've given you a chance to practice, my sons, so you know the general idea. Hold onto your hats for the real thing! I only hope you have the stamina – and the stomachs..." Ralphie slid a disparaging glance towards Talman, who blushed beet red. "We've got a long process ahead!" Ralphie's body snickered, with Lucifer's voice.

While the bodies of the selected damned shuffled their way, zombie-like, from the graveyard in a filthy procession of the living dead, the earthquake's effects had not ended with the uprooting of corpses.

Geothermal activity deep within the earth had cataclysmic effects upon the geological layers and minerals nearer the earth's surface. The shifting of tectonic plates induced a squeezing up of long inert gases and chemicals, forced up with the same strength as a volcanic eruption. Fortunately, much of this extreme activity and effects was buffered by the hard rock and layers of sediment above, but just as the graveyard and area around the obelisk had cracked and released deadly contents, so too did others.

There was a bubbling of black liquid from deep within the ground. To the uninitiated, to those who had ever watched *The Beverly Hillbillies*, or to those without a sense of smell, they might be forgiven for thinking that someone had struck oil. But it wasn't crude oil that formed *this* black gold. In fact, this particular black gold would buy only destruction, rather than contributing to the world's wealth. Bubbling up from beneath the ground, fountains of pure tar emerged: black, sticky and flammable, pooling in the lowlands to become deep tar pits that were forming along the hollow-surfaced areas around Tarklin and Melas. They sat, dark and sinister with potential disaster contained within them, each pool's area slowly growing as the tar gurgled and bubbled from its entry points at the bottom of the pits.

In the meantime, in the deserted towns, the after-effects of the previous storm and floods continued to devastate the urban centers within the surrounding countryside. As the floodwater settled and subsided, the damage caused to posts attached to live power lines and energy stations became evident and deadly. Combined with the spilling out of gas from washed out gas pumps in abandoned gas stations, and sparks from broken live electrical wiring and gas appliances, another kind of hell on earth let loose its vengeance. Fires spontaneously sparked, then caught, then erupted and swept quickly across the vast amount of debris left in the wake of the flood. Where the rush of water had stopped, and the destruction wasn't drenched, anything remaining dry rapidly became kindling for the fires that had broken out.

The sensations of the earthquake had not affected the outlying lands, so no one knew of the spreading tar pits. All attention was on the immediate towns, checking that the floods and fires were not endangering life. Dense smoke from the fires, and fog – a combination of the weather and evaporation of the floods meeting the fires – covered the valley between the two towns.

The Chief Fire Officer had made the decision only to attempt to keep the fires contained to the whole valley – a large area. They had evacuated and rescued all the townspeople they could, and he did not wish to risk his men's lives on saving the remains of flooded buildings. It was pretty hard to see from a distance, but his men on the ground ensured that there was no immediate danger. Whatever fire spread within the flood area would surely be doused by the floods soon enough.

Let Nature take its course.

Little did he know the new dangers that had occurred since any human life had set foot in Tarklin and Melas, and the damage that the earthquake had done – in more ways than one.

When the fires met the flammable tar in the ever-increasing pits and lakes of the stuff, the effects would be explosive – and even more catastrophic.

CHAPTER 14

As Jay, Jonathan, Amanda, and William approached the lobby, they immediately knew something was wrong. None of the hotel staff could be seen. The Stillwaters Restaurant was still closed and the hotel-resort, for all intents and purposes, looked abandoned.

The large television in the lobby was broadcasting everything they needed to know. Scenes of destruction and chaos were being displayed in vivid clarity and frazzled reporters were running around from scene to scene trying to document the live episodes.

Perhaps the most unsettling thing was when a reporter had the cameraman aim the camera into a pile of debris.

"This is utterly devastating," the reporter lamented on screen. *"What you're seeing behind me is the community of Big Issac. The entire neighborhood in ruins and – hey look – something is moving in the rubble."*

Suddenly screams could be heard off camera. The four in the lobby looked at one other, then back to the TV. Just before the camera feed was cut off, it caught the most horrific terror…

The word, "*Shit*," was screamed by someone off camera, followed by the camera dropping to the ground, but it was still rolling.

The reporter had been tackled and was on the ground – same level with the camera. A young child, gaunt and pale, was on top of the reporter biting his neck and face. Another walking corpse was grabbing the reporter from the side, biting at his ribcage and ripping whatever flesh it could with his dead, dirty hands. Several other "cannibals" quickly followed suit. They fell to their knees and joined the feeding frenzy. A piece of intestines was just being pulled into the air when the station cut to a commercial for some kind of dog food.

"Oh, my!" Jay exclaimed.

"Something bad is happening," Jonathan added.

"That would be an understatement," Jay replied.

This time, it was Amanda's turn to speak. "Jay, you have been very good to us, but I am going to need to ask another favor from you."

"Sure. Anything."

"About twenty miles north of here is the town of Clarksburg. That is where my house is – I think – unless it's been destroyed. Anyway, I need you to give us a ride back to town so that I can check on my house and at least try to get a grip on what's going on."

"Do you think it's safe?" Jay asked.

"Right now I'm not sure," Amanda replied.

"Lately, we have been surviving one day at a time," William added.

"I have no problem helping you guys," Jay said. "But, I would like to get some answers first."

William and Jonathan darted a quick glance at each other.

"We lost our footing and fell into the river last night," William fumbled out, assuming that Jay was wanting to know more about their fucked-up Huckleberry Finn-on-crack-style river rafting experience.

"All three of you?" Jay asked suspiciously. "I'm not buying it. Listen, I really need to hear the truth, no matter how unbelievable it is. Besides, the truth will set you free and if you tell what's *really* going on, that may shed some light on some things I've been experiencing."

"Jay, this area is overrun by vampires," Jonathan said matter-of-factly. "William and I have been battling them for years. Every time we try to escape, we are sucked back into this godforsaken place to fight them again."

"It keeps getting worse," William added. "And now, you're involved, Mandy." He looked sorrowfully at his aunt.

"Start from the beginning," Jay urged.

Jonathan carefully described the first night he met William. He detailed how he dropped off his girlfriend at the Melas Industrial Home For Troubled Youth where she worked one night when she called in for an emergency. He described how he saw a large, man-sized bat come flying down over the place and how he could not believe it at the time.

William then added his side of the story – about how he witnessed the brutal assault of the bat on the

Home's occupants and how he set the place on fire in order to kill the large bat.

Something about William's description of the inside of the Industrial Home bothered Jay. It was as if he was describing one of the scenes of his dream! *Could this all be related?!* Jay wondered.

"I had a dream the other night," Jay started. "Actually, I've had a bunch of dreams lately. They have been keeping me up – a lot, in fact. That's why I'm on vacation, to try to make sense of it all.

"But what you described sounds just like one of the dreams that I had. It was very terrible." Jay pointed to the television. "And those things – zombies or whatever they are – I saw those in my dreams as well. I can't even begin to think this craziness was real."

"It all started out with vampires," Jonathan replied. "However, I am afraid that the evil has gotten more sinister. It's almost as if hell is walking the earth. Something far worse than vampires are now out there – something from the water – those things are terrible beings, I tell you!"

"I don't know what is going on," William added, "but somehow, it's up to us to stop this!" William paced around the lobby and mumbled out loud. "But how? What would Jesus do if he were here?"

There was an awkward silence as each contemplated their next move. William looked like he was praying, with his head down. Amanda and Jonathan held hands and looked at each other with a mix of worry and affection.

"Well, it looks like I won't be skiing after all." Jay said.

Jay walked over to a stuffed bear that stood in the entrance of the lobby. The bear was standing upright – like a man – and one of the staff had positioned a Callaway Razr X golf driver in one of the bear's paws. Jay reached into the display and extracted the instrument.

"This might come in handy!" he exclaimed. "Folks, I think it's time to check out."

"You planning on golfing in the snow?" Jonathan mused.

"Something like that," Jay replied. "Guys, give me a minute to warm up the Mustang and when the coast looks clear, come on out."

Before the three others could reply, Jay had already left the hotel lobby and was heading out towards the parking lot.

Almost as if out of nowhere, a lurker walked in a non-human-like way. It was one of the zombies like the ones on TV. Jonathan, William, and Amanda gasped in horror as the undead creature moved at a quick non-even pace towards Jay.

Jay was surprisingly quick, however, and intercepted the creature with blinding speed, whacking it upside the head with the Callaway. The velocity knocked the zombie to the ground, but not for long. It grabbed for Jay's leg and Jay jumped away.

Jay pulled back and let the zombie have it again with the driver. This time, a big piece of brain and skull shot out from the zombie's head like grass and dirt from a golfer's swing when it connects with a ball. The creature stopped moving.

Jay made it to the Mustang and fired it up. It was very cold, but he didn't waste time getting it close to the lodge's door. The three others came running out.

"Hurry!" Jay exclaimed. "I don't know if there are more of them!"

As the Mustang sped out of the parking lot, one more zombie appeared from behind a tree. Jay hit it head on with the Mustang's front bumper and the creature rolled up onto the hood and smacked its face on the windshield. Luckily, the glass didn't break.

"Son of a bitch!" Jonathan exclaimed in shock and horror.

Jay slammed the breaks, causing the zombie to roll off the front.

He jammed the car in reverse and backed up about twenty feet.

The passengers all stared in amazement as the creature got to its feet and began a jerking walk toward the car to continue its attack.

"I seriously doubt this is covered on insurance!" Jay exclaimed as he put the car in first and floored it. A split-second before impact, he veered the car slightly to the left and caught the creature in the shin, knocking it away from the car.

They barreled out of there and headed for Interstate 79.

The team was silent all the way to the on-ramp.

Amanda was the first to break the silence. "What the fuck happened back there?" was what she managed to get out.

"Bad things," Jay replied. "Very bad things." He looked pale. "We are all about to be tested, I'm afraid."

"Hey, you're bleeding," Jonathan observed from the front passenger seat. "Did that thing bite you?"

"No," Jay replied, looking at the top of his right hand as it gripped the steering wheel. Fresh blood was oozing from a wound near his wrist. "It's an old injury. I must have busted it open when swinging the golf club."

"That's a relief!" William commented from the backseat. "If you'd been bitten, I'm afraid we'd had to use the club on *you*!"

"I've taken worse beatings," Jay laughed. "But I'm glad not to need my brains bashed in today!"

They all chuckled.

The interstate was open, but there were very few cars.

They made their way to U.S. Route 50 and drove into Clarksburg. Amanda lived in Locust Court, a community that jutted off Locust Avenue.

"So, is your street named after the short-horned grasshoppers?"

"What?" Amanda asked.

"Locusts – like the insects in the biblical plagues?"

"Oh, no. I don't think so." She replied. "I think the streets are named after trees."

As if affirming her assumption about Clarksburg zoning, the car left Route 50 and pulled onto the Chestnut Street exit. They passed Mulberry Avenue and came to Locust.

"Locust is a one-way street, so you'll need to go up to the next street and go around the block to get to my house."

Jay nodded and as they passed the Locust Avenue street sign, he slammed on the brakes.

They all stared at the street ahead and realized why he stopped.

Two blocks ahead, a horde of zombies had amassed in the intersection and were attacking anything in sight. These were the reincarnated dead from the city's two downtown cemeteries, hideously deformed from rigor mortis and eternally hungry. The downtown area of Clarksburg was a "no go."

"Oh shit!" Amanda exclaimed. "Listen, if we make it to my house I've got guns and that may help. Or, maybe not!"

Jay wasn't about to wait for the horde to get any closer. He quickly did a 180-degree turn there on Chestnut Street and reversed course. Not caring about local traffic laws, he quickly sped down Locust Avenue – the wrong way. "Now where's your house?!" he shouted.

"I live on Locust Court," Amanda replied. "One more block down."

Jay pulled the Mustang into her community and she quickly got out and ran to her house. "Wait right here!" she exclaimed.

"Sure thing, Mandy. Just hurry!" William urged.

The three males watched as Amanda rushed to her porch, fumble at her pockets and sprint back to the car. "Crap! Crap! Crap! I lost my keys! I have an extra set in my car but that's up in Canada!"

Jonathan was quickly reminded that just a day and a half ago, they had left her Porsche in the parking lot of a local motel in Ontario in favor of taking his truck. That seemed like ages ago in a different time.

"No sweat, sweetheart." Jonathan called out. "Do you want me to help you break in?"

She nodded affirmatively.

"Care if I borrow your driver?" Jonathan asked, gripping the shaft of the Callaway Razr that Jay had kept right beside them in the front.

"Sure thing," Jay replied. "Besides, I'm just borrowing it myself!"

Jonathan quickly got out and used the golf club to bust a piece of Amanda's first floor window. "I'll help you fix it, Sweetie, once we get out of this!"

Amanda simply nodded, climbed through the window and went around to unlock the front door. They came out quickly wielding a 12-gauge shotgun and a 9mm pistol.

"I have a feeling we're going to need these!" he said as he climbed in.

"So, you get everything you need?" Jay asked.

"Yeah," Amanda replied.

"Okay. Let's get to Melas and you guys can show me what all the fuss is about. Hopefully, we can settle this thing once and for all."

"That, or die trying." William added.

"I was afraid you'd say that."

By now it was 4:15 p.m. and the winter sky was already getting that dark hue of late afternoon. Also, a good portion of the zombie horde had made their way halfway down Locust Avenue and were only about a block away from where Amanda's housing development was.

"Looks like our path is blocked!" Jay observed.

"Turn left at the next street – that's Sycamore," Amanda called out. "Hopefully we can drive that down to Route 50 and avoid those ghouls!"

Jay nodded and drove the Mustang entirely too fast for comfort as they sped away from the all-devouring, flesh-and-brain-eating mob from Hell.

After a breathtaking high-speed descent down a very steep hill, the Mustang and its occupants made it back on to Route 50.

"Remember – go West!" Jonathan barely got out, helping Jay to avoid a wrong turn onto the east-bound ramp.

It took the team nearly twenty minutes to drive the ten-mile trek of expressway to Melas, mainly because there were several wrecked cars along the way and Jay had to carefully maneuver around them, at times following an access road to detour around the mess. Every time they left the safety of an open expressway to a more isolated access road, they all took a deep breath and wondered what other evils might be lurking just around the next bend.

By now it was getting dark again. The sun turned black like sackcloth as it disappeared behind the western sky. A full moon rose opposite with a blood-red radiance.

"This isn't good," William commented from the back seat. "This is just like the day we went to the Madison House, Jonathan – and in the same neighborhood!"

"Well, at least the Madison House is no longer there," Jonathan replied.

"Nor the obelisk, for that matter," William affirmed.

"But, regardless, I don't like going into that spooky town at night."

"I hear ya!"

"Honestly, guys," Amanda chimed in, "I don't think much quite tops the walking dead back there in Clarksburg."

"Point taken." Jonathan said.

As they approached the Melas exit, they were engulfed in a dense, fog-like mist that made it almost impossible to see even ten feet in front of the car.

Jay slowed down even more than before. "Folks, we might not see anything in this mist."

Melas was tucked in a valley and surrounded by several hills. Route 50 ran north of the town and when one turned off the four-lane, one got the feeling they were leaving the modern world behind and taking a small step back in time, or on this particular evening, akin to heading into a cloudy dreamscape reserved only for nightmares.

The mist gathered on the darkened hills like clouds of doom clinging to the shadows and the even darker woods behind it. Its evil knew no boundaries but drew all to the obelisk to play out whatever consequence would fall upon this night.

The Mustang's tires ran over something that was in the road. The bump felt unnatural.

"That wasn't a pothole," Amanda remarked in a worried voice.

"Probably a groundhog or a skunk," Jonathan said, trying to play down the possibility of something far more foul lurking in the mist.

The historical Fort Melas was nowhere to be seen. Jonathan knew its location – and that the Mustang was about to pass it. He just could not see it in the mist.

"Guys, it seems too early in the day for it to be so dark," Jay said. "His voice was firm and the others only hoped that he was not as scared as they were. Jonathan unconsciously stroked the pistol he was carrying trying to summon a mix between comfort and courage – none of the emotions he was feeling at the moment.

"Are you cocked and loaded?" Jay asked, looking at Jonathan and Amanda squarely.

Jonathan looked at his pistol. "Yes."

Amanda pumped her shotgun from the backseat. "Am now!"

The car struck something else.

William, who, like Jay, did not have a firearm, glanced around nervously. "What would Jesus do? What would Jesus do?" he mumbled repeatedly to himself.

Suddenly, there where zombies on both sides of the car pounding at the windows. There were at least eight of them and one under the car was somehow impeding the vehicle's ability to drive.

Jay yelled out, "I think Jesus would take those guns of yours and start pumping lead into some zombie ass!"

Amanda didn't wait for Jay to roll down the window or open the convertible top. She fired the first shot from her 12-gauge. The sound was deafening inside the cabin. The force of the shot blew out the Mustang's side window and effectively blew the head off of the ghoul closest to her.

"Holy shit, Mandy!" William screamed.

Jay leaned back and let Jonathan cross over him to fire a blast at the zombie on his side. Again, the sound was startlingly loud, but the crew managed to not be as surprised. Jonathan's bullet hit its mark as it blasted a zombie squarely in the chest. The zombie was knocked back, but only momentarily.

"Shoot him in the head!" Jay yelled.

Jonathan fired a second shot; this time it hit money! The zombie took the bullet right between its eyes and fell back to the ground immobilized.

Jonathan and Amanda poured out of the passenger's side and Jay jumped out of the driver's side. William stayed inside the Mustang and hunkered down in the back seat. This was mostly because he was the only member of the team who did not have a weapon. Jay, at least, had the golf club and that was better than trying to fight off the zombies with his bare hands.

The next eight minutes seemed like an eternity and shots rang out in all directions. William could hear the team working together as a unit – moving around the car together and attacking various zombies as they emerged from this mist.

Periodically, William would hear the dull, whacking-thud-like sound of the Callaway as Jay clobbered a zombie.

"Gimme a hand with the one under the car!" Jay called out.

William carefully looked up and saw Jonathan and Jay extracting the body of one of the ghouls out from under the Mustang. This was the one that had pinned itself under the car and made it difficult to steer.

Moments later they piled back into the vehicle.

Jay looked back at William. "The area's clear for now. Good thing you stayed inside!"

"Good thing that's all of them, as we're out of bullets!" Amanda exclaimed.

"Well, let's hope we don't see any more of those – things!" replied Jonathan. "Jay – are you sure you still want to see Melas?"

As they maneuvered around the now-truly-dead cadavers and up the first hill before the town of Melas, the group quickly understood that there was no longer a downtown area to drive through. The valley was littered with debris and there was truly no way the Mustang could go down there.

Just beyond the mist-filled valley where downtown Melas once stood and on the western hillside, a green pulsating light could be seen.

Jonathan and William shot a quick glance at each other.

"Isn't that close to where the Madison House was?" William remarked.

"Yeah," replied Jonathan.

Jonathan turned to William. "I've got a bad feeling that we might find the cause of all of this over at that light."

Jay raised his eyebrows and nodded.

"You obviously can't drive through town, but the backstreets up on the hills should get you there," Jonathan advised.

He pointed to a small side street that snaked its way behind the Melas Community College and near Jacobs Cemetery. Big chucks of earth had been busted open.

"Do you think those undead things came from here?" Amanda asked to no one in particular. She had grown noticeably pale.

"Probably." Jay answered.

William and Jonathan proceeded to tell Amanda and Jay the story of their assault of the Madison House – how they destroyed the obelisk that was erected in Mina Murray's yard and how it had "attacked" Father Alex's Ford Explorer, making it undrivable. They went ahead and told the entire story, how they had to walk the rest of the way up to the imposing Madison House and battle three vampires to their deaths.

"One of them was Miss Murray," Jonathan said and shuddered. "She seemed like a sweet girl the first time I met her – but not that night."

They had made it to the end of the flood damage and were on the other side of town.

"You're almost to Raccoon Run Road, but you still can turn around, you know," Jonathan told Jay.

"Let's make it quick," Jay said. "I've got a feeling that if we find out who's responsible for this – um zombie uprising or necromancy, or whatever it is – then perhaps we can put an end to it."

"Okay, Jay," Jonathan said. "But just so you know, my clip is empty."

CHAPTER 15

The vampire form of Jeff Abraham was driven by a force far greater than himself, and it was not only the burning hunger for blood. Like other creatures and phantoms now on the earth plane, he was magnetically drawn to the obelisk. It summoned him, and he was unable to resist. Not that he had the mind or any desire to resist such a natural, powerfully overwhelming urge.

So, through Tarklin, sustained by all the blood he could drink from the mobile blood donation van, and any living humans he might encounter along the way, Jeff Abraham was making his gradual way upstream on foot towards the obelisk, the pulsating throb of which mesmerized and sustained him like the beating of a heart. But night was upon him already and he was hungry once again.

His nose twitched. There was life here, someplace. He could smell it. His acute hearing picked up the sound of breathing, the gush of blood through veins and arteries, the opening and closing of valves in blood vessels. It taunted him in his hunger until he was crazed to seek its source and satisfy his craving.

He sniffed discreetly in the air, his sharp eyes hunting. He focused on a shack with a light glowing at the downstairs window. Within seconds, Jeff was there, crashing open the door and sinking his fangs into the neck of the redneck guy cowering behind the bed. He sucked the deliciously warm blood like an infant at a teat, but drew in bellyfuls of the stuff, draining the man dry and leaving his white-skinned body limp on the floor, glassy-eyed and dead. Sustained and satisfied, Jeff delicately wiped his mouth on the end of a bed sheet, then continued his journey to the obelisk.

He was not the only one making the grim, deadly pilgrimage to his glowing green destination. Staggering, stumbling figures of zombies – the Tarklin dead – joined him, a raggle-taggle procession of the undead, each with a single mindless mission. Every individual had lost its humanity, but each shuffled and softly groaned with its own ghastly regularity and rhythm, bodies jerking on their horrifying way – every one of which Jeff Abraham ignored as he pushed onwards, oblivious to everything but the need to respond to his Master's call.

***

At the shattered remains of the Tarklin Roadside Cafe, Rebecca Holbert and Deputy Cyrus Rose were picking their way through the wreckage, looking for other survivors. So far, there was no one else alive.

"Pa!" Rebecca called hopefully from time to time, unwilling to believe that her father might be dead. Little did she know that Parke had been the first to die, drowned out back of the Cafe before anyone else knew anything about the raging floods that had taken down the building and all within it in seconds. Still, Becky lived in rapidly diminishing hope that her father might have escaped death, and wouldn't give up until she'd found him.

So far, Becky and Cyrus had heaved aside large roof timbers, furniture, and wallboards to unearthed five dead. The speed and force of the torrential water and heaviness of the debris it had carried meant that they weren't just finding people buried or drowned, but in several cases, people were smashed beyond recognition, lying broken-boned in bloody floodwater with their brains and eviscerated entrails floating around them. Becky had thrown up until her throat was raw, and she had no more bile to give. But they persisted in the search, hoping that it might not be too late for someone under the rubble, if they could only help them in time.

"Christ, Becky." Cyrus wiped away the sweat from his forehead, and stood panting. He'd been drenched by the icy floods already, but the heat of his own sweat in the cold air was no compensation for the near-hypothermia. Their fingers were numb, and their entire skin a livid red with the freezing waters and biting cold. Becky stopped momentarily too, her eyes glazed with shock and despair.

"I sure could do with a good hot cup of your coffee right now, Becky!" Cyrus said wryly.

Rebecca barely registered his words, her eyes still scanning through the blackness of night across the wreckage for signs of life – or death. So, although she was staring in the right direction, her focus was on the rubble, and she missed the smoky, intangible wisps that flew through the night air with the directness of guided missiles, seeking their targets with unstoppable force.

But she thought she saw some movement: a flash of reflected moonlight, perhaps in one of the polished steel cooker splash boards – the cooker where her father was often to be found at work – and a shifting of one of the piles of debris. Distracted entirely from Cyrus, she took a few unsteady steps, picking her way through the jagged metal and smashed boards, over the rubbish in the direction she'd seen the flash of light and the slippage.

"Okay, Becky. Ready to go again?" Cyrus said, acknowledging that their momentary rest break was over. "Hey! I think I see a hand here!" Cyrus bent towards a pile of splintered plasterboard, lifting pieces of wood out of the way. "Whoa! Becky! Quick! We got a live one!"

The muddy hand, almost entirely buried, urgently scrabbled at the shards of board, and Cyrus began digging with renewed speed and motivation. "Hey, buddy! It's okay! We're here!"

Becky was fixated on the gleam of moonlight near the remains of the cooker, and the dark figure there: just a head and shoulders pushing itself up out of the mound of shattered building. Her eyes widened with hope and relief.

Cyrus was working hard to release the owner of the muddy hand. He flung aside a heavy length of timber, and underneath, from beneath the broken sticks of the Cafe building, a grotesque form burst forth.

"Holy Shit!" screamed Cyrus, unable to believe what he was seeing. It was barely human! A bloody mess of pulpy flesh and splintered bone was all that remained of a face. In fact, it was barely more than a smashed skull, with bloody shreds of skin flapping down, exposing mushed subcutaneous tissue, white daggers of bone, blood vessels and brain matter. Tufts of bloodied white hair, and an incongruous floral print dress and hand-knitted cardigan identified this horror as the bodily remains of Mrs. Muldrew, reanimated by the return of her damned soul.

The creature emerged from the pile of rubble like an explosion, scattering sticks and chunks of metal, and flew at Cyrus Rose, tearing at his throat with bony fingers. Cyrus had no time to scream before his vocal cords were ripped out and his carotid artery spewed a fountain of blood.

Despite having no facial features at all, the undead Mrs. Muldrew, without a mouth or teeth, her jaws and most of her front skull having been smashed by a flying timber, latched onto Cyrus' slashed neck with her gory flaps of facial flesh. A loud sucking noise could be heard, as Mrs. Muldrew consumed his blood, until the gross slurping was broken by Becky's scream.

Becky had rushed, slipping and clambering over the wreckage, towards the head and shoulders she'd fixated on, near the shine of stainless steel. But all around her, she heard the clatter and crack of shifting material and became aware of other figures eerily rising. Some came bursting out of the mounds with an explosion of wood and debris; others – the ones she and Cyrus had already unearthed and found to be dead, were simply heaving themselves up into a sitting position, and then finding their feet to stand.

All around Becky, the dark, shadowy figures of all who were dead surrounded her, and Becky had rapidly come to the conclusion that there was something very wrong with this scene.

Suddenly, she was assailed on all sides by a flurry of heavy, wet bodies that seemed to fly through the air. She felt herself in unimaginable pain, being torn apart and flung to the ground, with monstrous bloody creatures tearing at her flesh with teeth and claws; she saw a flash of Dave Snipe's face, but his dull eyes and snarl were virtually unrecognizable. Becky realized that she wasn't just being savaged: she was being eaten, and the pain was excruciating. It was no surprise to her, and even came as something of a relief, when she realized that she must be dying, and that this was the worst it could get.

***

After three hours of intensive necromantic ritual chanting by Ralphie and the others – involving blood-letting from Henry Cane and Talman Cane, dripping it onto crushed skull bones and the wood of coffins, and the consumption of goblets of blood – the full reanimation of recent corpses into zombies was completed, and the gateway to Hell was now open. Souls continued to fly like acrid fumes from the base of the obelisk, to seek reunion with their previous bodies.

All Hell was let loose.

Ralphie, Legion, Henry and Talman had completed their supreme ritual, and the droning of the obelisk, now a constantly pulsating and bright green, continued like a pagan chant.

Along the washed-out riverbed, heading back towards Floyd Lake, most of the zombies were still making their mindless journey towards the obelisk, ambling unsteadily and slowly, but Jeff Abraham was much faster. As a recently created vampire, unlike the ghouls, he still had the speed and flexibility of a fit human being. Also, he was driven by a stronger, more direct power, and therefore reached the obelisk long before the rest of them.

His impassive gaze scanned the area. Without either a human consciousness or a fully actualized vampiric presence, he was in a netherworld of transition between the two. Pulled in by the collective consciousness and the direct presence of Lucifer himself, he'd had no choice but to come here. Now that he was here, he had no consciousness of what to do next. He simply stood.

He didn't have long to wait. Henry and Talman Cane stepped out from their resting place in the bushes beside the obelisk, walked silently towards him and took Jeff by each arm. He allowed himself to be led directly in front of the obelisk and relented as they stripped him of his clothes in preparation for a necromantic ritual.

Ralphie and Legion stood watching and waiting. When Henry and Talman backed off, carrying away his clothing, Jeff stood naked before the powerful pulsating energy of the green glowing stone obelisk before him, and before the powerful demon and the Devil himself in their earthly garb of huge white bat and small boy.

Ralphie gave a sinister smile and surveyed Jeff Abraham appraisingly. He declared, "I have good plans for this one."

Talman and Henry looked at each another. Henry gave nothing but a blank stare, one eyebrow slightly raised behind his pebble-glasses, but Talman mouthed "What?" curiously. But Ralphie/Lucifer didn't elaborate or reveal what his plans were to the brothers. The Devil clearly had his own plans.

Only the Devil knew.

Another necromantic ritual was called for. Henry and Talman were near exhaustion by this point. The intensity and the level of magic they had been performing over the past few hours took a lot of energy out of them, and they were, after all, only half-human. Ralphie and Legion had boundless demonic energy that the brothers needed to call upon to feed off themselves, if they were to play their required role in the rituals of this most unsacred geometry, and survive this apocalypse when it came to full fruition. The End Times were coming, and they would need all their strength to fully experience and relish the events that were to come.

They had moved some boulders to form an altar-like table, the right height for Ralphie to reach across with ease, upon which they lay Jeff Abraham, face first. By now, Jeff was in a deep trance, which only increased when he lay down and submitted to whatever fate Ralphie had in store for him.

Ralphie raised his arms in the air and cried, in a patois version of ancient Aramaic and Latin: "Colpriziana, offina alta nestra!"

He then smeared Jeff with items of anointment symbolic of the four elements. His tiny hand wiped wet, muddy earth over the white skin of Jeff's still-muscular back, then patted on the tiny downy feathers of newly-strangled chicks, to represent "air."

He instructed the hypnotized Jeff to turn over. On Jeff's front, Ralphie splashed him with water, then patted on the ashes of cremated corpses to represent "fire." Ralphie stood back to admire his work, and smiled.

All the while, Talman and Henry stood a short distance away, swaying and chanting in Latin and Aramaic: "Colpriziana, offina alta nestra fuaro menut! We name Jeff Abraham, the dead which we seek, Jeff Abraham! Thou art the dead that we seek. Spirit of Jeff Abraham, deceased, you may now approach this gate and answer truly to our calling! Berald, Beroald, Balbin, Gab, Gabor, Agaba! Arise, we charge thee and call thee!"

They had begun the process, but their acute senses were alerted to the sound of possible danger. Their ritual was interrupted by the distant sound of an approaching car. All of them stopped, glaring with anger, and Ralphie hooked his head, giving the great bat, Legion, an implicit instruction to find out what was going on.

Legion raised his huge white, sail-like wings and flew up the hill to the perch where the Madison House once stood, to look down over the valley to see who it was that was approaching. It was very hard to see anything with the still-hanging cloud of foggy mist, and Legion's beady eyes in this bat-form were not ideal. Bats, after all, are blind, and find their way by radar. Even with his supernatural senses on hyper-alert, the fact that he was effectively in the physical form of a bat meant that his sight was limited, and he couldn't see through the fog.

"Hide him. Quickly!" shouted Ralphie angrily, and sprinted off as fast as his little legs would carry him.

The ritual was only partway through, but with impending danger approaching, Ralphie made a run for it, disappearing into the woods behind the obelisk to search for incoming back-up troops from his own zombie legions. They really should be arriving by now in their hundreds, and soon his power would be at its maximum. Ralphie needed to see for himself the assembled undead, to calculate how soon he might strike, and fully engage in The End Times. He therefore went to check on the progress of the zombie army who were amassing in the valley-crater of the newly emptied Floyd Lake.

Who knew who was in the approaching car? It could be State Troopers – the National Guard – the police! Henry and Talman had to act fast. The Cane brothers dragged the now unconscious naked, muddy and dusty Jeff Abraham into the weeds and bushes to hide him until whatever snoopers had gone.

They innocently stepped out into the clearing in front of the obelisk, dusting off their suits, raking their fingers through their hair and straightening their jackets, ready to welcome their visitors. Whoever they might be.

CHAPTER 16

"Oh my God!" cried Jonathan, staring through the windshield of Jay's Mustang, expecting the obelisk to be just as they'd left it: broken into pieces; destroyed. But there it was: large as life, standing tall, its sharp point skywards, and seemingly... alive.

"But I thought... What's happened?" William gasped, amazed.

Jay pulled the white Mustang off the road and onto a dirt patch that indicated the start of the driveway to the old Madison property, not far from the glowing obelisk. Jonathan and William jumped out of the car, crazed with horror to see the obelisk now rebuilt and in full power, its eerie green aura pulsating. There was no one else around, just the throbbing granite-like stone, illuminating its surroundings with a repetitive pulsation of green hues.

Amanda joined them at their side, and said softly, "Shit. What does this mean?"

William exclaimed, "How did this happen?"

Jonathan's eyebrows frowned, as he set his teeth grimly, "How the Hell. That's how."

Above them on the hillside, a fair distance away from the obelisk, but still reflecting the light emanating from the stone, there was a flash of movement and

214

color. Like a pale, lime green ship's sails, for those inclined to look up, there was a glimpse of a large bat, its wings stretched out as if forming a huge wind-break.

Jay spotted it, jarred into action. He leaned out of his driver's side window and told the others, "I'll take care of the bat. You stay here and I'll be right back!"

"Bat?"

As Jay started to pull out, Amanda reached in through his rolled-down window, aiming to place her hand on his steering wheel to momentarily stop him and say one last thing – but she accidentally caught the car horn instead. It blew loud and clear, and she recoiled in alarm.

"Well, Gabe, you blew the horn!" Jay commented strangely to her. "So I guess the party's over! I'll see you on the other side."

Before she could react, he sped off up Raccoon Run Road toward the cul-de-sac at the top of the hill, while William was frantically tugging at Amanda's hand to drag her closer to the weird monument.

"The obelisk! We destroyed it – smashed it up!" William cried in shock, hurrying forward, pulling his aunt along behind him.

"Well, you didn't make a very good job of it," Amanda commented.

"It was smashed to pieces when we left it!" William persisted, catching up with Jonathan, who strode ahead. "Father Van Helsing told us to destroy it, so we did, and we..."

"Never mind that," Jonathan said sternly, "Whatever happened – it's back. Looks like it's rebuilt itself – or been rebuilt."

"Maybe it's not real. A projection or a hologram or something?" William released Amanda's hand and ran over to the obelisk to investigate.

"Willy!" Amanda yelled, horrified and fearful.

All eyes on the obelisk and William's mad dash towards it, no one noticed the two evil brothers, lurking idly in the shadows of the trees in the old Madison backyard, merging the blackness of their souls into the black of the shady depths.

William came to a sudden stop in front of the stone, his arms outstretched. He reached out his hand to touch the obelisk and there was a shocking, blinding flash that lit up the area. A bolt of white lightning had burst from it, shooting William backwards so he was flying through the air, his arms and legs loose like the limbs of a puppet with its strings cut, until he fell with a sickening crunch into the yard.

Amanda screamed, her initial cry of warning turning to a frightened shriek as she saw her nephew thrown across the yard to land immobile and senseless on the ground. Immediately, she and Jonathan rushed to William's aid, horrified and afraid. William lay crumpled on the ground, not moving, and was either unconscious or dead. Jonathan reached him first and sank quickly to his knees over his body.

"Oh, my God! Oh, my God! Is he breathing?" squealed Amanda, still running towards them, as Jonathan opened William's collar to check his pulse, bending close over the boy's body.

When Talman Cane kicked Jonathan hard in the head, this unexpected blow hurt him badly. Taken completely by surprise, with all his defenses down as he gently tended to William, Jonathan literally didn't know what had hit him. He felt the extremely painful blow, was propelled sprawling sideways, and his vision failed him as his head spun and he saw stars.

Henry grabbed Amanda from behind, wrapping his right arm around her neck and digging his forearm into her throat, choking her and dragging her down. He flung her backwards over his bent knee, aiming to push her into the muddy ground. But with a fury and determination beyond her strength, she quickly twisted herself around as she was overturned, and while falling, she succeeded in kicking Henry Cane in the groin. In fact, she succeeded in stamping her booted heel hard into his most vulnerable spot with all her might, as he stood with his legs wide and braced against overbalancing as he threw her over his knee. Cane fell backwards himself, with a pained groan, Amanda sprawled beside him.

Jonathan could hardly see, his head still spinning with disorientation. His breath came raggedly as he desperately fought off unconsciousness and whirled his arms blindly and wildly to fight off Talman's attack. Talman, standing over him, and fully in control, still had the upper hand. He kicked him again with savage accuracy – this time in the solar plexus. Jonathan doubled over, exhaling hard. He'd had the wind completely taken out of him, and lay breathless and choking, almost blacking out. He could not fight.

Talman grabbed him by the hair and painfully dragged him with supernatural strength across the yard. He jerked him upright and pitched him forward at the rear of the yard – pushing him over the crest of the hillside, through some soft weeds and bushes. The hillside was steep there, and a body flung down rolled at speed, like a log, crashing through the rough grass and brambles. Jonathan helplessly rolled down, spinning dizzily for about forty yards; his arms and legs flailing uselessly, before eventually his body came to a stop, by crashing into some trees, which broke his fall at last.

Just below him, where he lay inert, the moans of zombies could be heard. The sound signaled the fact that the gray, undead army was growing closer, making their unsteady but unfailing lumbering walk to assemble their forces, as commanded by the collective consciousness initiated by Ralphie and Legion. They were somewhere close by, and getting closer.

Amanda saw this all happen within a second. She sat gathering her breath, struggling to get up onto her feet from beside the howling Henry Cane, who was clutching his crotch and recovering from her sharp boot. But in that moment when she saw Jonathan's body hurled down towards the distant ghoulish moaning, she screamed in fury. Her nephew might well be dead, and here was her lover – tossed over the hill, most likely broken-boned zombie fodder by now. Her emotions were at the highest pitch; extreme, incensed anger and grief stoked a fire within her she had no way of controlling. The blood within her was rising to a boil, but there was something else, even more powerful and inexplicable. Her eyes completely changed to startling blue, glowing brightly, signaling that something – a power beyond comprehension – was close to coming forth.

Henry Cane took his opportunity and punched her violently in the face. With barely a flinch, she punched him straight back with a hard blow that sent him stumbling backwards in the driveway, shocked and astonished.

Talman arrived back and tackled Amanda like a linebacker, taking her by surprise and wrestling her to the ground before she had a chance to respond.

Henry lunged forward, grabbed her arms and yelled to Talman the words that chilled her blood: "Rape her, brother!"

***

With his eye on the looming white creature at the apex of the higher land above him, Jay Christiano had put his foot down on the accelerator so hard, he had spun his wheels in the mud to get to the top of the hill. Fortunately his high-quality tires had bit, and gained purchase, and the Mustang's purring engine responded well, driving him fast towards his destination. And now that he was almost there, heading for the cul-de-sac, which served as a turning spot for cars, he had actually lost sight of the great white bat he pursued.

"Where is it?" he muttered through gritted teeth, peering through his windshield and windows.

A massive crashing blow above his head signaled his answer, as the metal frame of his soft-top roof buckled around him, and the vicious talons of the bat tore through the leather and cloth cover, inches from Jay's head. Legion had flown upwards a short ways, silently taking off on his great wings, disappearing above Jay's line of vision and he now descended on to the top of Jay's Mustang, sinking his claws into it and seeking to rip off the roof to get at the driver.

Reaching the cul-de-sac on top of the hill, Jay did a series of handbrake turns, spinning the car in fast motion, skidding round and round the turning circle to dislodge the huge bat. It swung round precariously, holding onto the roof frame, its huge bony-skeletoned white wings wrapped around the car, obscuring Jay's view. He sped a few feet, then slammed down on the brake to throw the beast from the car, and watched in relief as the gray-white flurry of fur, fangs and leather jerked over from the roof, hurtled down the windshield and bounced off the hood onto the roadway in front of him.

Without a split second's delay, Jay stepped hard on the gas, pulling forward fast, to drive over the giant bat. With a bump and a sickening crunch, followed rapidly by an unearthly screech, Jay positioned the car's front tires over the beast's wings, pinning down the creature splayed to the ground, just the edge of his moist fur body beneath, and his horrid, rabid head freely jerking this way and that.

"Aargh!" there now came from Legion – a roar of anger, more than of pain.

The car rattled and Jay felt the car tremble. It was repeatedly lifted slightly up and down, but the demon's furious attempts to buck the car off, like a raging bronco ridden by an implacable wrangler, were to no avail. The strong but delicate hollow-boned framework of his wings was broken, their power lost, but the great bat body was still attached to them, and they were wedged under the wheels and body of the car.

The bottom of his ugly gray-furred body flailed helplessly under the bumper, his furious fanged mouth opened wide, while his head thrashed from side to side, growing exhausted from the exertion.

Jay casually got out of the car, slamming the door with a movement that vibrated the whole car and made the demon wince with pain.

"You damaged my new car," Jay began. "I am not happy."

"Fuck you!" screeched Legion, "that's the least of your problems! Hahaha!" he laughed grotesquely, his twisted bat-mouth cruelly exposing his vicious fangs, dripping with saliva.

Jay remained unfazed. Somewhere in his consciousness, part of him sat back and observed himself in wonder. He hardly knew himself these days, but was driven by some kind of natural inevitability. All was as it should be, and he sensed a calm knowing within that he could not explain. It was as if he had found his true purpose in life. This was meant to be, whatever was happening – and he reacted instinctively, naturally, to these extraordinary events, knowing exactly what to say and do.

He knew not how.

Jay took a couple of steps onto the dead, leathery wings, looking down at the butterflied bat underfoot. He leant back on the hood of the car, making Legion suck in his breath, hurting with the added weight. Jay half-sat, leaning back, folding his arms loosely across his chest, and crossing his ankles, as if stopping for a friendly conversation with the mechanic who lay checking out his car's undercarriage.

"So, Legion, powerless at last..."

"Haha! Not powerless! I can still call upon the elements to break your bones, human! You will die! And then you will be just another damned soul in our employ, facilitating the End Times! Haha!"

But then, despite his cruel laughter, something inside the demon wondered, *How does he know my name?* A chill fear suddenly ran down his broken spine, alerting all his senses and suspicions. Who was this strange human, fearless in the face of a demonic force, manifested as a massive, monstrous bat? Legion had seen humans who were more afraid of a tiny moth than this man was of him, now. Something was not right here.

With all that remained of his strength, Legion summoned up his demonic energy and began to curse up a storm that would blow this small man off the hillside to his death. He took as much of a deep breath as he could and began chanting an invocation to the powers of evil to rise up a storm.

He intoned deeply with his rich baritone, "Ri! Iri! Riri! Briri..."

"Remember when I threw you to the pigs and you drowned?" Jay stated calmly. Legion stopped in his tracks, mouth open in fear and realization, as Jay continued, shaking his head sadly. "When will you realize that you cannot beat me?"

Legion froze in shock, his eyes boggling.

Shit!

Jay disappeared around the side of the car away from Legion's sight, and the great bat lay his head down on the ground, bewildered. His beady eyes shot sideways, back and forth with reptilian fear, trying to make sense of it all.

He was terrified.

This was a strange human emotion he had never experienced before in all his millennia of life and half-life. It was an emotion he didn't like. He didn't want to feel it, and to his horror, this very sensation of extreme terror was increasing, and adding to it, panic, anxiety and impotence. It was an unexpected cocktail of unwanted feelings that sapped all his manipulative Machiavellian energy out from his mind, just as much as his physical powers had left his body.

Legion felt the car rock slightly from a shifting movement inside, and the slam of the trunk again made him wince with pain, as the shock of the vibration reverberated through his body. Then he heard an odd buzzing sound. Just a couple of seconds of loud buzzing, like a thousand angry hornets; then it stopped.

Jay appeared again in Legion's sightlines, holding a bright yellow DeWalt cordless reciprocating saw that he had retrieved from the trunk of his Mustang.

"Whoa! No!" Legion exclaimed, trembling, his beady bat-eyes wide with fear: "Look – I'll give you anything you want! We can work together. You'll be a Prince amongst..."

Jay's determined glare blasted the last vestiges of Legion's negotiating skills right out of the water. Jay approached, crouching down on his haunches and pressed the trigger, starting up the powerful buzzing motor.

"No! Wait! Let me talk to you..." Legion yelled, above the noise. He strained his head further and further away from the blade, which was moving so fast that it appeared invisible, but he was ultimately unable to escape.

"I think the time for talking is over," Jay said simply.

There was a limit to how far Legion's bat head could reach in his attempt to escape the inevitable. Ironically, he exposed more of his neck by extending it away from Jay and his reciprocating saw's voracious blade. Pinned to the ground by the car wheels standing on his outstretched wings, Legion lay crucified and helpless. The rapidly sawing blade was approaching slowly and precisely towards him in the steady hands of Jay Christiano.

"This is for my Father," Jay said.

"We can..." a tortured scream cut off Legion's desperate last words. The soft, light breeze of the blade's movement near his neck, accompanied by the buzz of the saw's blade, became a firm pressure onto the skin. The saw bit through it, then sliced through flesh and cut further on and deeper, into muscle, vocal cords, arteries and veins. Jay blinked against the shower of liverish flesh shreds and blood that sprayed up into his face. As it hit the vertebrae, the blade stalled and began to resist, but with a gentle adjustment of the cutting angle, it then buzzed slowly through the bone, with a grim crunching sound as it went. Legion was now silent and still; his eyes dim and clouding with death.

Jay proceeded to continue sawing off Legion's head, his mouth set in a grimace of concentration, blood spattering his clean clothes and leaving tear-shaped red drops on his cheeks and beard. This time, he was killing the demon once and for all.

***

Talman knelt painfully on Amanda's shins and tore at her clothes. Meanwhile his brother pinned her wrists down on the ground, her arms stretched above her shoulders, while she struggled wildly, growing more and more angry.

"I like 'em feisty," Talman hissed in her ear. He taunted her, adding, "I am going to do you in front of your dead son's body while your dead husband is being eaten by zombies!"

At this point, Amanda simply snapped. To say she "saw red" would be wrong: she saw a strong, passionate and powerful blue color, which affected her like a transformation of indescribable brilliance.

Giving a throaty and bestial roar, which gradually transformed into a clear-as-a-bell single musical chord of beautiful vocal harmony, a blindingly bright, blue-white light shot forth from her body, which grew suddenly taller, stronger, and luminescent, of itself. It completely emanated, and in fact, appeared to be made of, a pure blue-white light that shone almost as strongly as the sun.

Huge white, sparkling, crystalline, yet powerful wings sprouted from Amanda's shoulders and a great chorus of celestial reverberations burst out from the air around her. She was transfigured into a powerful angel of incredible beauty and awe-inspiring grandeur.

Henry was startled beyond sense by this occurrence, and he released his grip on her arms. Or rather, he opened his hands in amazement, as her body shot up, not only to her feet but grew to at least twice her normal height. Talman and Henry stood horrified, shielding their eyes from the blazing glory that Amanda now was.

Amanda, in fiery angelic form, seized this opportunity to lean down and grab a hold of the dumbstruck Talman, and before he had time to struggle or anyone even knew where she was going, she flew with him in her hands, lifting him like a toddler, up to the top of the obelisk. By now, she was a full-fledged angelic being, twelve feet high, with supernatural physical power and strength. She drew back her arms, holding the small man higher still, with Talman too shocked even to struggle, and with incredible force and strength that would not be humanly possible, she impaled him stomach-first on the obelisk's sharpened, uppermost point. Talman's body shook with a death-rattle before he gave up the ghost with a quiet groan that seemed to be almost a gasp of relief. His limbs and head hung limply above the scene, draped over the highest sides of the obelisk, while the cruelly pointed shaft stuck out of his spine, black with his wet blood, which dripped down the side of the obelisk and pooled at its base. There it slowly sank, absorbed into the churned up soil, merely darkening it, but otherwise leaving no trace.

Although Henry's attention had been occupied by the incredible, awful celestial sight before him and the horrifying fate of his brother, from the corner of his eye, Henry saw movement. He turned his head sharply towards the backyard, only to see William stirring: unbelievably, he had heaved his head and shoulders up from his prone position, and was now leaning on one elbow, gathering his resources to sit up.

The boy is still alive!

Henry's sharp Machiavellian mind sparked into using this fact to his advantage. He rushed over to the yard and lunged himself behind William. He pulled out a pocket knife, holding it to William's throat.

"Stop right there, Fae!" he warned, as Amanda landed lightly back on the ground, and stopped a few feet away.

Amanda screamed as Ralphie – now fully transformed into Lucifer, in his fearsome demonic form of horned, black, two-legged beast with cloven hooves – grabbed her from behind. With his powerful pincer grip, he had grabbed her by the tender point near the collarbone, ripping through her shoulder with his taloned fingers – breaking bone and flesh – and driving her to her knees.

"You fool!" he scolded Henry, in a booming voice that shook the ground. "This is no fairy! This is the Archangel Gabriel! No mortal can fight her and expect to win!"

"Lucifer, let me go!" Amanda commanded in the thunderous voice of the Archangel.

"No, no, Gabriel," Lucifer replied. "You killed my son and you expect mercy? I will delight in killing off your puny human female avatar and sending you both to hell to see how the other half live! The time for my reign over the earth is *now*!" The whole valley and hillside rang with the sound of his voice, "And you are too late to stop it!"

Henry laughed and cut William's throat with one slick slice, dropping him back to the ground.

"No!" Amanda/Gabriel roared as William fell.

Lucifer jabbed a fist through Amanda's angelic back and it came clear out through her chest. Her lifeless form dropped forward, but Lucifer swept her up and tossed her body on top of William's.

"What a distraction," Lucifer touted idly, and then dismissively spat on the two bodies with hacked up phlegm from his evil throat. "And a terrible loss of Talman," he lamented.

Full force in the face, almost knocking off his head, a log swung hard like a baseball bat hit Lucifer so surprisingly and suddenly that it dropped him to the ground, stunned unconscious and immobilized. Jonathan had climbed back up the hill during all the commotion and he had struck hard and fast.

Jonathan then turned to Henry and whacked him across his arms, which he had raised defensively in front of him, to protect himself. The still-bloody pocket knife flew out of his hands and across the grass, while Henry hardly knew if his arm was broken or just badly hurt. One hand swung loose at the wrist, for sure, and he couldn't feel his right arm at all.

Furious and venting his grief over William and Amanda, Jonathan swung the log again, striking Henry across the other shoulder. Henry cried out in pain, both arms now disabled and useless. With another swift and heavy swing from Jonathan's bat, the last Cane brother was helplessly flung onto his side on the ground, unable to use his arms or hands to push himself up.

Quickly taking his opportunity, Jonathan proceeded to raise and hammer down his weapon to beat Cane again and again, smashing his bones with the log-bat. He aimed for his head, and heard a crack as his skull presumably split inside. With the next blow, his skull crumpled and the skin split open, the shards of broken skull-bone releasing spongy brain matter, like lumpy gray porridge. One of Cane's eyes dripped out of the broken socket in a smashed, gelatinous mess, and blood flooded from his ears, broken nose and mouth.

Jonathan had no sense of overkill. In a split-second he had recalled all that was bad about the Cane brothers, and thought only of vengeance for William and Amanda, whose own broken bodies lay heaped nearby. Then thought and mind gave way to pure brute violence. So, long after Henry stopped moving, Jonathan persisted in beating his inert body. He was frenzied and unstoppable, and would have continued indefinitely, had he not been disturbed by a greater problem.

Jonathan had succeeded in mashing Cane's brains out, and turning Cane's head to a complete pulp of red, pink, bloodied gray mush and splinters of bloodstained white bone, before Lucifer recovered, only a minute or two after he had been struck down.

In one swift movement that darkened the skies and simultaneously filled it with bloody fire, Lucifer overwhelmed the landscape as he opened his crimson and ebony wingspan to its full twenty feet, and stood in all his shining demonic glory in front of the obelisk. At the same time, the earth shook deeply, and Lucifer gave a great, sonorous, incredibly loud roar.

Shit.

Jonathan realized that his solitary moment of surprise was over and that he was terribly outmatched: by the devil himself. As Lucifer fixed him with blood-red, burning eyes, the demon started to charge at Jonathan, his cloven hooves ready to pound away from the uneven soil and grassy hummocks towards the yard, his dragon-like wings folded tightly to prevent slowing him down in the wind across the driveway.

"Oh, Jesus. God help me!" Jonathan cried, concluding that his final breath must be only seconds away. He felt faint and lightheaded.

Then, like a white horse galloping to the rescue, through the clouds of mist and smoke, Jay Christiano's Mustang flew off the hill, driven at full speed, and barreled into Lucifer at over one hundred miles per hour, crashing into the obelisk.

It smashed it to pieces, exploding the car on impact and sending the entire evil set-up over the hill. Like a giant fireball, Lucifer, the obelisk and Jay's Mustang flew, aflame, into the muddy crater of the emptied Floyd Lake below. The first strike was tremendously explosive, blowing up the lake into a volcano of fire and smoke. Like a match struck to ignite touchpaper, and then setting off a chain of fireworks for an elaborate choreographed display, the series of recent tar pits caught and were one by one set on fire.

Many of the zombies had already gathered there at Floyd Lake: almost the entire undead army's forces had waded through the tar pools and oily mud to assemble as instructed.

Within seconds, the explosive fireball had set off a flaming conflagration, fueled by the highly flammable tar. In the lake bed the idle and repetitive moans and groans of the walking dead had become ear-piercing shrieks and screeches as the ragged zombies with their dried skin and wasted bones began to roast and char like firewood.

Unearthly cries, fit to chill the soul, emanated from every single member of the stumbling hordes, who staggered blindly into one another like walking human torches. Some of the recent dead's fresher flesh and layers of fat were melting like wax and burning with a lively, strong yellow and red flickering flame; the older dead and the longer aflame were smoldering and burning to a cindery red more swiftly, their limbs soon falling into piles of charcoal twigs and gray ashes.

The dried out lake hollow was now the Lake of Fire, and the tar pits were soon great red subsidiary fires themselves, below the hills.

Above it all, in the short distance between the yard and the old site of the lost obelisk, Jonathan had taken a few stumbling steps forward. Devoid of all adrenalin, Jonathan's heightened emotions of extreme grief, fury, fear, and despair sucked the rest of life out of him. His physical exertion from the climb of the hill, the frenzied attack upon Cane and the sideswipe at Lucifer had used up all of his energy. Only adrenalin and determination had kept him going, and all that was gone. Willy... Amanda... all gone. His battered body, hurt dreadfully from the downhill fall, had taken its toll, and his head injuries were severe. Hardly knowing if he was alive or dead, or just dreaming a terrible nightmare, he gave in to oblivion and passed out.

CHAPTER 17

Amanda's story:

"Gabe, you bit off more than you can chew, old friend. You and your child need to take better care of yourselves. Perhaps you should go to Phoenix – a nice desert town."

"My name is Amanda." she replied. Jay simply looked into her eyes and smiled. "And William is not my son," she added. "He is my nephew."

"I know that," Jay replied warmly. "Besides, I always think of William by his angelic name 'Michael.' I'm talking about your other child." Jay lovingly touches her stomach. "Yours and Jonathan's."

"What?! I'm confused." Amanda replied.

"Rest for a while. You had a long night. Besides, your husband needs you for his recovery."

Amanda started to protest, "We're not married..." and then drifted off to sleep.

William's story:

The last thing William McConnelson, III remembered before passing into the darkness was a bolt of severe pain shooting through his arm and pushing him backwards through the air just as if he had

233

placed his hand on a live high voltage wire. He landed on his back at least that much he knew.

At some point later, he sensed movement. He was moving, or more accurately, he was being moved. Dark shadowy figures had appeared out of nowhere and were dragging his body down into some kind of hole – a well perhaps?

He tried to breathe and could not. Something about his throat. His mouth was filled with the coppery taste of blood, yet his limbs were paralyzed and he felt helpless to do anything about it. The shadowy figures had come for him and all he could do was lay there!

The shadows began to curse him and bite him all over. William had never been bitten by another human being before, but now was traumatized at how bad it felt. The shadow creatures appeared to be human except for their sharp fingernails – which resembled claws – and their pointed teeth. They wore no clothes.

"You're Satan's now, priest!" one of them jeered.

William started to cry. "G..g...god!" he tried to get out, but was having difficulty speaking – somehow his vocal cords had been severed.

"You're god can't save you!" one of his tormentors said as it bit into William's calf. "No one can save you now!"

They continued to drag him into the hole, which he now realized was the obelisk inverted into a downward-pointing vortex plane going into the ground. The air had become rancid and excruciatingly hot. It was a stark contrast to the damp winter-like weather he had been enduring the past few days. But right now, he would give anything to be back in the snowy mud of

West Virginia rather than this dark land where it was very, very hot. He could smell the sulfur in the air but still could not breathe. He was very afraid. *They're dragging me to hell!* he thought.

Without the physical capacity to speak or move, cold panic washed through William. *This is it! I'm going to be spending eternity in this shadow-land. Will I end up as one of them?* he wondered, thinking of the demonic souls that were attacking him.

He no longer had the capacity to think. All of the prayers he learned in Catholic school completely left him and he became too scared to even remember his name. Somehow, the only thing that crept into his mind at the time was the first couple words of a child's song. *Jesus loves me... mmm...mmm...mmm.* That's all he could remember – no other words but *Jesus loves me.*

"God damn you priest!" one of the shadow figures – the one who had bit his calf – chided. "When will you give up?"

Strangely enough, the figure backed a few inches away from his leg.

William repeated the song in his mind again, *Jesus loves me.* And again – over and over in his mind.

The tormentors all had backed off slightly, but continued to wail verbal curses and assaults at William.

William was barely aware that they all had released their grip from him when he added to his song/prayer, *Jesus save me!*

"Recognize this?" came a voice from out of nowhere.

William turned his head to see a tall figure standing next to him holding the head of Legion – the big bat.

The shadow-creatures shrieked in terror and began to run. He threw the decapitated head of their demon leader at them as they jumped into the hole made by the obelisk and disappeared from sight.

"Jay?" William said confused, suddenly able to speak. "What's happening?"

"You are in the outer darkness. The angel could not come with you to this place; but your eternal spirit is here now," he said. "What once was broken has now been restored." He reached down to the ground and helped William to his feet. The deep bite wound on his calf also began to heal and strength started returning to his body.

A brief but vivid memory came immediately to William's mind. He saw a shining blue angel being held from rescuing him just as his throat was cut. *Mandy?!*

"Oh, no....wait! I died. I'm dead?" William said in a voice just above a whisper, the gravity of the circumstances sinking in.

"Yes. Gabriel did not reach you in time and Michael's power was bound to the physical plane the moment you touched the obelisk.

"These things are beyond your understanding. But in time, you will learn."

William could tell that a bright white light glowed from around Jay, but everything else was pitch black. He felt safe, but at the same time worried.

Jay looked at William, studying him, and added, "Jonathan is hurt badly. He will need your help."

"But how can I help him, if I am here?" William was filled with anguish because of what he just experienced.

"Don't be afraid," he said, "for you are very precious to God. The Archangel Michael chose you as his vessel to battle Satan on the Earth. Gabriel chose Amanda.

"Satan and his spawn were terribly powerful. You fought the good fight, but died."

He smiled as he looked into William's pleading face. "Sometimes I give people a second chance. More often than not, it would seem."

"You are not Jay Christiano, are you?" tears of recognition streaming down his face.

"At least you have my initials right," he said as he hugged him. "Now. William Michael McConnelson, III – WAKE UP!" he shouted.

William blinked and was suddenly back in the driveway of the Murray House on Raccoon Run Road.

"Wake up, Willy! William. Please, wake up!" Amanda pleaded with him. "Jonathan's hurt!"

EPILOGUE

Somewhere along U.S. Route 50 West, a lone drifter staggered along the edge of the highway. Something happened to him, but he didn't know what. He had an ungodly headache and was terribly nauseous. Had he been poisoned? Where was he anyway?

It was very dark. The drifter walked a little further, stumbled, and hit his head on a post holding up a highway sign. He let out a sigh as he raised his head to see what it was he ran into. He could barely make out the words "Dark Hollow Road Next Left" in white letters on a green background.

Something happened there, but he couldn't quite remember. It was in the news. Oh well, it didn't matter – he wasn't going there. The night was dark enough the way it was. Mumbling something to himself, he put one foot in front of the other. "Go west young man!" he joked to himself, not really sure why he was saying it.

The night air was cool and in the distance he could hear thunder. A storm was approaching. He walked about a half mile more before the first droplets of rain began to fall.

It was going to be a long night.

A semi truck roared past the drifter at an unfathomable rate of speed. It was several hundred yards past the drifter before it slammed on its air brakes, creating a thunder of its own as it came to a stop. The drifter was grateful and hurried up to meet the truck.

The semi was painted black with red flame stripes. Normally it would not have been visible on a night like this had it not been for white LED lights that were placed along the tractor-trailer's side. The license plate simply had the numbers "309" on the back.

The drifter opened up the passenger's side door and looked into the cabin.

Behind the driver's seat was a large man with a heavy red beard. He was wearing a red and black flannel shirt that reminded the drifter of a lumberjack. "You're going to catch a death of a cold out here with it starting to rain and all. Get in."

"Much obliged," the drifter said, pulling himself into the passenger's seat.

As the drifter closed the door, the truck screamed back to life and began its rapid acceleration westbound.

"I'm Big Joe," the trucker introduced himself in a courteous greeting. "You look kind of familiar. You from Melas?"

"Melas?" the drifter asked, confused.

"Yeah, that town back there."

"I don't think so," he replied, not completely convinced in his answer.

"I ask that because I'm from that town and you looked like a guy I went to school with many moons ago. Your name wouldn't happen to be Jeff Abraham, would it?"

"No sir. But you can call me Victor."

ABOUT THE AUTHOR

Gary Lee Vincent was born in 1974, in Clarksburg, West Virginia, where he lives with his wife Carla and daughter Amber Lee. He is a graduate of Fairmont State University and Columbus University. Vincent holds a Ph.D. and M.S. in Computer Information Systems and a B.S. in Business Administration Management and Psychology.

He is a real estate developer, entrepreneur, author and recording artist.

His interests include music, travel, photography, technology, art, and of course, creative writing.

ALSO BY
GARY LEE VINCENT

GARY LEE VINCENT

PASSAGEWAY

OTHER GREAT TITLES FROM

Burning Bulb

PUBLISHING

WWW.BURNINGBULBPUBLISHING.COM

THE
BIG
BOOK
OF
BIZARRO

JAM PACKED
OVER
50
WEIRD TALES

EDITED BY
RICH BOTTLES JR. AND GARY LEE VINCENT

WESTWARD HOES

9 Weird Western Tales

FEATURING THE NOVELLA
"BIG TROUBLE IN LITTLE ASS" BY WOL-VRIEY!

EDITED BY

RICH BOTTLES JR. AND GARY LEE VINCENT

Creators of The Big Book of Bizarro

RICH BOTTLES JR.

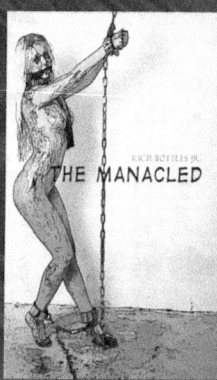

WEST VIRGINIA
HUMORROROTICA

BOSTON
P
O
S
H

WOL-VRIEY

VEGAN

ZOMBIE

APOCALYPSE

WOL–VRIEY

www.ingramcontent.com/pod-product-compliance
Lightning Source LLC
Chambersburg PA
CBHW071138170626
46809CB00002B/668